About the Author

Camilla is an engineer turned writer after she quit her job to follow her husband on an adventure abroad.

She's a cat lover, coffee addict, and shoe hoarder. Besides writing, she loves reading—duh!—cooking, watching bad TV, and going to the movies—popcorn, please. She's a bit of a foodie, nothing too serious. A keen traveler, Camilla knows mosquitoes play a role in the ecosystem, and she doesn't want to starve all those frog princes out there, but she could really live without them.

You can find out more about her here: www.camillaisley.com and by following her on Twitter.

@camillaisley
www.facebook.com/camillaisley

Also by Camilla Isley

I don't WANT TO BE FRIENDS

JUST FRIENDS BOOK 4

CAMILLA ISLEY

Dedication

To all brothers who loved the same girl…

One

David

She wasn't coming.

David cast another furtive look at his watch. At a quarter past eight, Haley was an hour and fifteen minutes late. No, not late, because she'd never meant to come. Earlier, the whole "meet me, I'll be there waiting for you regardless" bit had seemed a wonderful idea when he'd proposed it to her. Teasing. Romantic. At least, when he'd been so sure she'd show up. Now, he'd turned into a sorry dude: David—*Pathetic*—Williams, stood up by the girl of his dreams, drinking alone in a bar.

What a waste of a Saturday night.

David had come to The Plough and the Stars early. He'd ordered his first beer at six forty-five and drank it in small sips, pacing himself, not wanting to be tipsy when Haley arrived. His second beer had gone down a lot faster. By now, he'd lost count of the rounds.

"Can you close my tab?" he asked the bartender.

The bartender nodded efficiently. He walked to the cash register and came back with David's credit card and a bill to sign. David wrote his name on the receipt, his handwriting more flourished than when he was sober. Then he stumbled off his stool, drained the last two inches of lukewarm beer in his glass, and dropped it on the counter with more force than he'd intended.

"Sorry," David apologized.

The barman curled his upper lip and gave David an unimpressed look as he swiped the glass off the counter without comment, probably accustomed to sloppy drunks.

Taken aback by the barman's evident contempt, David's hands curled into fists as icy rage flooded his system. He was itching for a fight, but the last lucid part of his brain nagged at him that causing a brawl in a bar near campus was not the smartest idea. And he wasn't really angry at the bartender, anyway. A pair of green eyes flashed in his mind. No, he was definitely mad at someone else.

Outside the pub, hot air dripping with humidity blew in David's face, doing nothing to help him sober up. Why did Boston have to turn into a swamp every August? With a disgusted wince, David stared up at the brick buildings of Cambridge, trying to orient himself. After taking a few tentative steps up Massachusetts Avenue, he realized he was heading the wrong way and turned around, dragging his feet all the way home.

David was no less drunk when he unlocked his apartment door twenty minutes later. He careened inside the house and realized at once that something was off. *Different.* David frowned, unable to identify what was wrong, but definitely sure something had changed since he'd left earlier that night. He scanned the living room and kitchen area for a clue, but everything seemed just as David had left it.

Then he saw it: Scott's door, an inch ajar. That door had remained firmly shut for the past two months. David narrowed his eyes and walked toward his brother's room. Pushing the door open, he saw a huge suitcase parked next to the bed. His worst fears confirmed: Scott was home.

His brother was back in Cambridge from his summer internship in California a week early. Why? And where was he now, if not here?

David's body reacted to the answer an instant before his brain connected the dots. His heart contracted in a spasm, and he missed a breath. There was only one place Scott could have gone: to see his girlfriend. Haley.

"Ooooh, perfect." A bitter sneer spread on David's lips. "Welcome home, brother," he said to the empty room, and then punched the door with so much force that the skin on his knuckles split. His opponent—*the wooden door*—took the hit and bounced back with no lasting damage sustained. The same couldn't be said for David's fist.

With a throbbing hand, and a dark mood none improved after the punch, David stumbled over to the freezer. As he took out a bag of frozen peas and applied it to the back of his hand, his gaze landed on a bottle of vodka sitting at the bottom of the compartment.

Like most drunk people, the idea of getting even more trashed was incredibly appealing to David.

He dragged the bottle out, smiling. "Hello, baby," he told it. "Why don't we keep this party going?"

With the bag of peas precariously balanced on the back of his injured hand, David dropped the bottle of vodka on the kitchen counter and went hunting in the cabinets for shot glasses. He found six and arranged them in an orderly row on the countertop.

One-handed, he opened the bottle and poured the first shot, saying, "For my brother." Then he poured another. "And his lovely girlfriend, Haley. I wish them a happy life together." Each statement was followed by a shot glass being filled. "To myself, for playing the part of the fool again. And to Brigitte, who tried to teach me a lesson many years ago I don't seem to want to learn."

David stared at the one remaining empty shot

glass, trying to decide who he should dedicate it to. Unable to come up with another toast, he shrugged. "To me again, because I'm worth it."

David filled the last glass and threw the empty vodka bottle into the sink, where it landed with a loud clunk. Unmoved by the noise, David lifted the first glass and toppled the contents into his mouth. One by one he brought the small glasses to his lips, banging them on the counter once he'd downed them. The vodka burned his throat as he swallowed, and it spread like acid when it reached his empty stomach. But David didn't stop until all the glasses were dry, by which point he was irredeemably intoxicated.

Head spinning, he staggered to his room and, fully-clothed, fell face-down on his bed and passed out.

Madison

Madison woke with a groan, the morning light burning through her closed eyelids. Why could she never remember to close the blinds? Not that hard, right? All she had to do was turn the stick and the slim metal panes would seal themselves off, keeping the light out and allowing her to enjoy a Sunday morning lie-in. But, no, she always forgot, and those rotten, pupil-stabbing sunrays woke her up at the crack of dawn, *pronto.*

Pity, she'd been having the best Scott dream ever. Right before she'd woken up, he'd walked into her bedroom, ripped off his shirt, and told her he wanted her.

"Ah, hell," she huffed, throwing off the sheets and getting up.

Now that she was half-awake, the building pressure in her bladder became too strong to ignore. Barefooted, garbed in only a matching pair of pale pink panties and a flimsy tank top, Madison dragged her feet off the bed and headed for the apartment's shared bathroom.

Madison was too busy rubbing the sleep out of her eyes to pay much attention to where she was going. So, she was utterly stunned when she almost crashed nose-first into someone walking out of the bathroom. Someone really tall, and mostly *naked.*

Madison's jaw dropped as she stared up into Scott's emerald green eyes. He was standing in front of her, bare-chested and wearing only a pair of unbuttoned jeans, with an apologetic smile stamped on his sexy lips. Exactly as he had in her dream.

She blinked.

Am I still dreaming? Isn't six in the morning a little too early to start hallucinating?

"Hi," the hallucination said, in a fantastic impersonation of Scott's low, masculine voice. "I thought no one would be up this early." Imaginary Scott proceeded to fasten the button on his jeans, visibly embarrassed.

The pull was inexorable, and Madison's gaze was drawn to the gesture. Her eyes traveled down his flat-muscled chest, skimmed over a sculpted, rock-hard six-pack, and came to rest on the deliciously inviting V of muscles disappearing below the jeans waistband.

Mmm, Madison thought, chewing on her lower lip. *Well, if I really have to hallucinate something, high-five, imagination.*

"Madison?" the hallucination asked. "Are you all right?"

"Never been better," Madison said, smiling like a fool.

"Oh, okay." Imaginary Scott shifted on his feet.

Madison didn't care if he seemed uncomfortable; this was her dream, so she might as well take the lead. She raised her hand and splayed it across Imaginary Scott's chiseled chest. But when her fingertips came in contact with warm, living flesh, Madison gasped and retracted her hand as if burned. "You're real!"

He chuckled. "Last time I checked."

"But you're in California," Madison protested.

"I came home a week early to surprise Haley," Scott—the real, not one-bit Imaginary Scott—said. "Sorry if I startled—"

"Oh, gosh," she interrupted. "Oh… oh." Shocked, Madison pressed one hand over her mouth while the other moved down to cover her panties. Oh dear goodness, she was standing in front of Scott wearing close to nothing and acting like a complete fool.

She flushed red head to toe, and, following her hand with his gaze—*his turn to gawk*—Scott's cheeks pinked as well.

With another awkward smile, he repeated, "I thought nobody would be up this early… Sorry."

Madison couldn't take a second longer of this exchange. She pushed past him, muttering a hurried, "Excuse me," and barged into the bathroom, locking the door behind her.

Breathing heavily as if she'd just run ten miles, Madison rested her shoulder blades against the wooden door. *Crap. Crap. Crap.* She hit her head back against the wood in time with the imprecations. Then she realized Scott might be able to hear her and stopped before she made an even bigger fool of herself.

She took long, steadying breaths, trying to slow her heart down. But the stubborn idiot seemed to be settled on run mode, making her gasp like there wasn't enough oxygen in the room.

Embarrassment and shame burned a steady fire in her lower belly.

Madison collapsed down, her butt hitting the cold tiled floor, while a million thoughts crossed her mind.

Scott was back. He'd just seen her half-naked, hair disheveled, and probably sporting a horrible case of morning breath. Madison exhaled into her cupped hand and smelled it.

Shit.

What the hell was Scott doing in her bathroom at six in the morning?

He must've spent the night here, making love to Haley in the adjoining room while Madison had been sleeping next door, clueless. And they'd probably make love again soon.

Double shit.

This last image lit a different kind of fire in Madison's guts. Flames of anger and disappointment. Flames of envy flaring into hate. Hate for the best friend Madison couldn't legitimately hate, and hate for herself for all these contrasting feelings that kept eating at her.

And now there really wasn't enough oxygen in the room, maybe not even in the entire apartment. Madison needed out. She used the toilet only because her body forced her to. Then she turned the lock and opened the bathroom door a crack, poking her head out to make sure the hall was clear. Scott was gone, so she sprinted back to her room, pulled on a pair of sweatpants and a T-shirt, grabbed her gym bag, and fled.

The campus gym ran various group classes, and Madison was hoping to burn off her bad mood with something up-tempo and high-intensity. But the only thing on this morning's schedule was Hatha Yoga. Madison scoffed; she wasn't in the mood for anything relaxing, calming, or even remotely of the feel-as-one-with-the-universe philosophy. She needed to drive her body to its limits, so she wouldn't have any energy left to think about what had happened—or to imagine what might be happening at this very moment in Haley's bedroom.

Head bent low so as not to make eye contact with anyone, Madison jammed in a pair of earbuds and stepped on the first available treadmill. She set the machine on the longest and hardest program and selected a random cardio workout playlist on Spotify. But even with her feet flying on the mill and music pounding in her ears, Madison's brain was still functioning at full capacity, damn it. And her heart, despite being busy pumping blood at 160 beats per minute, still had time to break over and over again like it had been doing for the past eight months. Eight long months since the day Haley had come home from Hawaii and announced she and Scott were an item.

How much pain could a broken heart cause? There had to be a limit…

Because I can't take this anymore, Madison thought.

Scott's two-month internship in California had put a false sense of security in her. With him gone, away from Haley, it hadn't been so bad. There had been no sudden stabs in her chest when she ran into him on campus, or when she caught an intimate stare between him and Haley—or, worst of all, when she saw them kissing.

With Scott and Haley's relationship on hold, Madison had coddled herself in the false idea that she was getting over him. That these stupid feelings would go away. That she wouldn't feel so damn miserable all the time anymore.

Nope. Not for you, Madison. Not a chance in hell.

This morning's encounter with Scott had been the proverbial cold shower, her false sense of security promptly washed away. The illusion she wasn't in love with Scott gone.

So, what now?

Alice's words from their last "Scott" discussion echoed in her mind. *"Listen, Maddie,"* Alice had said. *"Who knows if Scott and Haley will stay together, or if you'll ever get to be with him, or even want him anymore? You could meet someone who'll sweep you off your feet tomorrow... And our lives are going to be so completely different in a year when we graduate, anyway. You just have to be strong and pull through."*

Alice was right. All Madison had to do was to be strong and pull through. She'd already suffered eight months of this. She could survive twelve more.

I can do it!

I have to be strong and pull through, Madison repeated inside her head. Eyes focused forward with a newfound determination, Madison pumped up the speed of the treadmill and ran and ran and ran toward the new finish line she now saw standing before her. Graduation was only a year away. Her life would change. Everything would change. And she'd be finally free...

Two

Haley

"I may have traumatized one of your roommates," Scott said playfully, snuggling back under the covers next to Haley.

"What do you mean?" Haley asked, still groggy with sleep.

They had done little *sleeping* the night before, and Haley wouldn't mind staying in bed for another month. All she wanted to do was to drop her lids, burrow closer to Scott, and rest.

"I bumped into Madison on the way back from the bathroom. It was… awkward."

That woke Haley up, all right. She was so tired of the guilt tainting her relationship with Scott. But whenever Madison appeared in the picture, she couldn't help herself. After discovering Madison was secretly in love with her boyfriend, Haley had sworn never to spend the night with him here, in the adjoining room to Madison's. She'd vowed to do everything humanly possible to spare her best friend's feelings. But last night had been so unexpected… spontaneous, unplanned. Her happiness at seeing Scott again had obliterated all other thoughts. Scott had come back to her; nothing or no one else had mattered.

"Why? What did she say?" Haley asked.

"Not much. She made some weird comments; she was probably still sleeping. When she realized she was standing there in her underwear, she locked herself in the bathroom."

Great. Haley groaned inwardly. *I spend one night here with Scott and, of course, Madison had to bump into him the next morning.*

The front door slammed shut.

"Think it's her leaving?" Scott asked. "I hope I didn't offend her. I assumed no one would be up this early."

"Don't worry." Haley turned and wrapped her arms around his neck, dropping her head on his chest and deciding to postpone the drama. Right now, all she wanted to do was enjoy her boyfriend being back after so many weeks apart and not brood over anything else, period. "I'm sure she's not offended."

***

Several hours later, when the need for food overcame all other base needs—namely, sex and sleep—Haley and Scott finally emerged from her room, both completely dressed this time.

Alice, her other roommate, was in the kitchen making a sandwich, and when she spotted Scott her eyes widened. "Oh, hello! When did you get back?"

Scott waved. "Just last night."

They hugged. "Tired of all that sun and palms?" Alice joked.

Scott let Alice go and wrapped an arm around Haley's shoulders. "More missing what was at home."

"I bet." Alice nodded understandingly. "You guys want a sandwich?"

"Actually…" Scott scratched the back of his head. "I'd better go home, I barely set foot in last night. I don't even think David knows I'm back."

David.

The name sent a chilly current coursing down Haley's spine. Their text exchange from last night scrolled through her mind.

Want to grab a
beer later?

It's not a date

Okay, Miss Robot

Let's do it this
way

I'll be at The
Plough and Stars

The Irish Pub
down Mass Ave.

At around 7

If you feel like
joining

You know where
to find me

I'm not coming

I'll still be there

In case you
change your
mind

I won't

Never say never

Gotta get back to
work now

See you later?

Dammit. Had he been waiting for her all night? Well, she'd told David she wasn't going, but he hadn't believed her. And the truth was she would've gone if Scott hadn't shown up unannounced on her doorstep. Haley imagined David waiting for her at the pub alone. She pictured his expression changing from cocky self-assurance when he first arrived, to bitter disappointment—*anger?*—as time passed and she didn't show…

"Hey, are you okay?" Scott asked her, frowning slightly.

"Yeah," Haley said. "Just a bit lightheaded. We skipped dinner *and* breakfast."

"Right. I got so used to skipping meals at the hospital, I don't even notice anymore."

Alice arched a brow. "Aren't doctors supposed to promote a healthy lifestyle?"

"Besides being the worst patients, they're also the worst role models for a decent life-work balance," Scott said. "All right, I'm going." He leaned in to kiss Haley on the forehead. "And you girls, don't forget to eat your vegetables," he joked.

They all laughed, and Haley walked him to the front door.

Scott paused on the threshold. "I'll call you later, okay?"

"Mmm-hmm."

He gave her a soft kiss on the lips and left. Haley shuffled back to the kitchen, climbed on a stool, and dropped her head on the bar.

"Sandwich?" Alice asked, somewhat sarcastically.

"Yes, please."

Haley heard a plate being placed next to her face and Alice climb on the stool beside her, but still, she didn't rise up.

"Okay, what's with the desperation act?" her roommate asked. "Aren't you happy Scott is back?"

"Yeah," Haley groaned, finally straightening. "Of course I am."

Alice made a "So what?" face.

"It's just that everything around us is so complicated."

Alice took a bite out of her sandwich and waited for her to elaborate.

"This morning Scott walked out of the room for like… five seconds, and he bumped into

Madison."

"Oh."

"From what I gathered, he was half-naked, and she was half-naked, and she didn't take it very well. I always try not to sleep here with him. But last night…"

"It's okay, Haley." Alice nudged the plate toward her. "Eat up. Madison knows you're with Scott. Okay, bumping into him out of the blue might've been a shock, especially if she was wearing only underwear—you know how shy she is—but you have to stop the guilt tripping. You're doing nothing wrong."

Haley chewed a bite of her tuna sandwich and found it difficult to swallow.

"What else aren't you telling me?"

"David."

"Mmm… Not overjoyed his brother is back, huh? He had you all to himself for two months."

Alice's words stung a little. "What's that supposed to mean?"

"Listen, Haley, I'm not Madison, and I have no beef with David, but even a blind person could see you two got close over the summer…"

"So?"

"I don't know." Alice shrugged. "You tell me, you brought him up."

"He asked me to go out for a drink yesterday, as friends…"

"And?"

"I said I wouldn't go, but he's impossible. He told me he'd be waiting for me anyway."

"And were you going to meet him?"

Haley nodded.

"And that's when Scott showed up on your doorstep."

Haley nodded again.

"And David spent all night waiting for you in a bar… And, let me guess, you feel guilty about that, too?"

"I do. It's like wherever I turn, my relationship with Scott is hurting someone. I'm uncomfortable here because of Madison, and now it'll be horrible at his place, too, because of David."

"So David makes you uncomfortable… how?"

"Not you, too."

"Sorry?"

"First Madison, then my mother, and now you. I'm tired of people asking if I have feelings for David."

"Well, do you?"

"I just said I don't want to talk about it."

"But I think you do, and I'm the right person for the job."

"Why?"

"I'm on your side. I don't care which Williams brother you date, and I don't care if you have feelings for both. Correction, I *do* care, because you're my friend, but I don't judge. You wouldn't be the first girl who has feelings for two guys, and I'm not trying to be your moral compass, only a friend."

"Okay."

"Would it be easier if I asked questions?"

"Yep."

"Okay, let's start with the easy ones. You don't hate David anymore, right?"

Haley tried to fly back in time three months and summon up all the anger and contempt she'd felt whenever she'd thought about David… The jerk who'd treated Madison like a doormat. The lying bastard who'd made Scott accept the internship in California. But all those hard feelings had been gone for a long time.

"No."

"And you consider him a friend, at the very least."

"Uh-huh."

"But he likes you."

"It's a little more complicated than that."

"How?"

"He… might've said he's in love with me."

Alice's eyes bulged out. "What? When?"

"Over the summer. Remember the mega storm right before the term ended?"

Alice nodded.

"He told me standing under the rain in the

middle of Harvard Yard."

"Romantic much?"

"*Notebook* worthy."

"And what did you say?"

"That I love his brother."

"Oh, harsh! And he…?"

"Promised he'd wait for me. For when I was ready to admit I have feelings for him, too."

"Well, I guess that brings us to the only question that matters. Do you have feelings for him?"

Haley stared at her lap, shaking her head. "I wish I could tell you 'no' and mean it. But the truth is I don't know anymore. The only thing I know for sure is I want to be with Scott."

Alice took her hands. "Well, then there's only one thing you need to do."

"What?"

"Make David understand that's where you stand, with no more room for interpretation. It'd be cruel to give him false hope. Have you been one hundred percent clear with him?"

"I—I…" Haley scrunched up her face into a dubious expression. "Ninety-five percent?"

Alice squeezed her hands, giving her a *"make sure you close that five percent gap"* stare, and Haley nodded. She'd have to talk to David as soon as possible. What a great conversation to look forward to.

Scott

Scott entered his apartment and immediately caught a whiff of an out-of-place smell that, if he had to define it, he'd name: House After a Rave Party Eau De Toilette. But it made little sense; David wasn't the type to throw house parties, and the place was too clean for a party to have happened recently, anyway.

After dropping his wallet and keys on a low cabinet, Scott moved into the kitchen to get a glass of water. Here the stench worsened, the after-party smell mixing with the distinctive funk of something rotting. A quick glance around the kitchenette, and the source of the mystery stink was easily explained.

Six empty shot glasses stood arranged in a neat row on the counter. Scott lifted one and sniffed it: *vodka*. So, apparently, his brain associated vodka with house parties. That made sense. But the weirdest discovery was a bag of frozen peas left unopened to melt under the direct sunlight filtering in through the window.

Scott picked the bag up, which went all limp and mushy in his hand, and he had to suppress a gagging reflex as he sealed it inside several trash bags. He closed each up with three or four tight knots to prevent the stink from coming out and dropped the bundle into the bin. He'd take it downstairs later.

What the hell had happened here? Why would David get drunk on vodka and leave a bag of frozen peas to rot on the counter? Sometimes his brother was really mysterious.

After opening the window to let fresh air in, he stacked up the tiny glasses and dropped them in the sink, where he found an empty bottle of vodka. Yeah, David must've had quite a night. Shrugging, he threw the bottle into the glass bin, rinsed the glasses, and put them in the dishwasher. Then he decided he'd better check on his brother.

David's door was ajar, and Scott approached cautiously. If David didn't know he was back, he could have a girl in there. Why use *six* shot glasses unless he was playing some sort of game? David wouldn't be drinking that much on his own, would he? Six vodka shots seemed a bit over the top even for him. But a quick peek inside David's room confirmed that they were alone in the house.

His brother was lying on the bed, face down and fully clothed—white T-shirt, jeans, white sneakers—very much with the air of someone who had drunk half a bottle of vodka on his own the previous night.

He lay so still that Scott wondered if he was breathing. A soft poke to David's side produced a loud snore, confirming he was alive. Scott shook his head. *What the hell, bro?* He seriously considered leaving David "as is," but then he'd just be bothered by the image of his brother's poor bedding situation.

So, with a sigh, Scott decided to undress him using a bottom-up approach, starting with the shoes. Mid-disrobing, he noticed the swollen, caked-in-dried-blood knuckles of David's left hand. Had he been in a fight? With whom? Scott shook his head and continued rolling David left and right to remove his clothes. When he had him in his boxer briefs and T-shirt, his brother finally stirred awake.

"Scotty," David said with a slur. "Welcome home, brother."

Scott struggled with David's limbs to tuck him under the sheets. "Missed me?" he asked sarcastically.

"Threw a party in your honor last night."

"Really?"

"Yep, I had so much fun."

"I see," Scott said, playing along. David was too delirious right now to be making any sense. "How about I get you an aspirin?"

"Stop being so fucking nice," David said, angry all of a sudden.

His brother struggled to straighten up, but as soon as he managed to right himself into a sitting position, he must've become dizzy because he collapsed back on the pillow.

"I don't feel so good," David concluded.

No shit, Scott thought.

"Wait here," he said. "I'm gonna get you that aspirin and something to clean the hand."

Without waiting for a reply, Scott moved into the bathroom, took the pills and disinfectant out of the cabinet above the sink, and returned to the kitchen to get a glass of water. Before heading back to David's room, he grabbed his phone out of his pocket and dialed Haley's number.

Haley

"Miss me already?" Haley said, picking up the phone.

"Yeah, of course," Scott said.

"But that's not why you called."

"No, it's that… I don't think it's a good idea for you to come here tonight. I know I just got back, but—"

"Why?" Haley asked, her stomach contracting with a sneaking suspicion.

"It's David." Scott sounded worried. "I've never seen him like this."

The knot in Haley's guts tightened. "Like what?"

"He's stinking drunk, and he's babbling about

throwing me a 'welcome home' party last night. Totally insane. All I can tell you is that I found an empty bottle of vodka in the sink and David passed out on his bed. I think he got into a fight with someone."

Haley swallowed. Oh gosh, it sounded worse than she'd thought. If David had known Scott was back, he'd also have known why she'd stood him up last night.

"In a fight?" Haley asked. "Why would you say that?"

"Because his right hand looks like he's put it through a meat-grinder."

"Oh."

Haley couldn't explain the injury. She only hoped David hadn't done anything stupid.

"Listen," Scott continued. "I'd better go check on him, but you stay home. He's already moody enough. One second he's all peace and love, and the next he gets angry for no reason. David's not a very good drunk."

No kidding.

"Okay," Haley agreed. "I'll see you tomorrow, then?"

"Yeah, I'll call you when I wake up. Love you. Bye."

"Bye."

As Haley hung up, the front door opened and Madison walked in.

Oh, hell… let's jump from one broken heart right onto the next…

"Hi," her roommate said, smiling.

Not the reaction Haley had expected.

"Hey?"

"So big surprise last night, huh?"

Madison was acting as if she didn't care at all. She was all sparkly eyes and bright smiles, making Haley's chest surge with gratitude. Madison really was the best friend in the world. If their parts were reversed, Haley wasn't sure she'd be able to be so gracious.

"Yeah." Haley finally allowed herself a tentative smile. "Heard you had a little surprise yourself this morning. I'm sorry, I—"

"Oh, that… Pffff…" Madison waved her off and turned to hang her bag on the rack behind the door. "I'll admit I wasn't expecting to run into Scott…" Madison kept fidgeting with the bag a while longer than necessary. *To hide her face while she talked?* "It was… weird. Didn't expect a boy in here. I was half asleep and probably made no sense."

Madison turned at last, pink cheeks bright with embarrassment, but softened by a no-big-deal smile.

"So you're not upset?" Haley asked.

"No. Nooo. I mean, it *was* awkward…" She shrugged. "But that's it."

Madison's eyes sent Haley a clear message that her friend probably wasn't able to express in words—a silent plea of *"Can we pretend this never happened and that I'm not in love with your boyfriend?"*

Haley nodded, agreeing to Madison's unspoken request. Deciding to change the subject, she said, "Hey, what are you doing tonight?"

"No plans yet. There's a book presentation at a bookstore downtown I'd like to see, but I don't feel like going all the way to Boston alone."

"Why don't we go together? We can hit the event and then stop for a bite somewhere."

"Are you sure?" Madison looked hesitant. "Don't you want to be with Scott?"

"Scott's having David problems."

"David problems?" Madison frowned. "Already?"

"Uh-huh. Let's get ready first, and then I'll tell you everything?"

"All right. Meet here in twenty?"

"Yeah." Haley pulled Madison into a hug and added, "Thank you."

"For what?"

"For being the best friend in the world." Haley held her tighter.

Madison squeezed hard, too, and in that simple gesture, they shared another million unspoken words.

Three

Haley

By the next morning, Haley was dying to see Scott and itching to learn if David had pulled any more drunken stunts. She woke up way earlier than usual for a non-school day and managed not to call Scott right away. For the better part of the morning, she kept herself busy with mundane tasks she usually postponed until they became super urgent. She sorted the alarming pile of both dirty laundry—*to wash*—and clean laundry—*to put back in the closet*—she had accumulated before visiting her parents, then cleaned her room and emptied the suitcase she hadn't had a chance to unpack yet. She figured she might as well get all those things sorted before school started and she got too busy.

But when by eleven-thirty Scott still hadn't called, Haley's patience had officially run out. Her bedroom was cleaner than when she'd first moved in, and she'd even done the kitchen and bathroom. With no more housekeeping distractions available, she grabbed her phone and called her boyfriend.

Scott picked up after several rings, his voice

sounding all groggy with sleep. "Morning."

"Morning?" Haley said jokingly. "It's almost noon."

"Hey, I'm jet-lagged."

"You were in California, not Japan."

"Still, it's only barely past breakfast time for me."

"Luckily for you, I love brunch. Want to grab a bite together?"

"Sure."

"Should we go out or stay in? I mean… is everything okay over there? Is David okay?"

"Mmm… I have no idea, I'm still in bed. Hold on. Let me check."

Rustling, scuffing noises cracked out of the speaker as he got out of bed. Then the sound of a door opening, footsteps, another door, footsteps again… and, finally, silence.

"He's gone," Scott announced.

"Gone? Where?"

"To work? His internship shouldn't be over yet."

Haley had no trouble believing that. From the way his boss had made David slave over work assignments every single weekend for the past two months, it made sense they wouldn't let him off until the very last day of summer break.

"Is he going to be okay?"

"I suppose. He slept all of yesterday and I

made him drink two bottles of Gatorade, so he should be fine. Except for that hand, maybe."

Haley hoped so. For now, physically "well enough to go to work" was all she wanted to hear about David; she still wasn't ready to investigate his bruised ego, or worse, broken heart.

"So what do you want to do for lunch?" she asked. "Should I come over?"

Haley was already warming up to the idea of an empty house and Scott all to herself, when he said, "Why don't we do something outside? I've spent the last two months locked in a hospital with artificial air and artificial lights. I could use a day outdoors."

"You want to go hiking or something?" Haley asked, unconvinced.

The great outdoors weren't exactly her thing.

"How about the beach?"

"The beach? You've turned surfer boy on me. Err... you do realize we're in Boston, right? Not exactly famous for its beaches."

"Come on, who cares? Yesterday I looked up a few spots we can check out. I just want to spend a few hours with you, relaxing in the sun and doing nothing all day. No brothers, no roommates... only me and you."

"Well, when you put it like that." A wide smile spread on Haley's lips. "Give me half an hour."

"Okay, come here when you're ready. My

place is closer, and we have to take the Red Line at Central."

"I'll buzz you when I get there."

***

The trip to the beach turned out to be longer and sweatier than Haley would've liked. It took them about forty-five minutes and one T line change to get to Revere Beach. But nothing could dampen her good mood. Scott was here, they were together, so who cared where they went or what they did?

As expected, the beach was nothing special—a thin strip of sand just off the road, with nondescript concrete buildings in the background. But at least the ocean was blue, and the place brimmed full of people. The waterfront closer to the road had been fenced off to make space for a sand sculpting competition. Different teams of four to six people buzzed around with various tools, busy building impressive sand structures of sea monsters, buildings, ships, people, and many others. Food trucks lined the back of the fenced area, the smoke drifting up from their grills and permeating the air with the delicious aroma of smoked meat. And off in a corner, at the end of the sculpture display, a band was playing live on a stage.

Haley and Scott walked by the various sculptures, admiring the works of art and marveling at the level of detail the artists were able to impress on the sand. When they reached the final sculpture, a mermaid sitting in an open shell, they bought a pair of Chicago-style hot dogs and found a spot at the edge of the crowd to settle down on the beach and eat with more privacy.

"Mmm, so good," Haley said after her first bite. She eyed the overflowing toppings and sauces incredulously. "I mean, it should be disgusting, but it's delicious."

Scott laughed. "It really should be disgusting."

Haley licked her fingertips after finishing the last bite. She watched Scott shove the rest of the hot dog into his mouth and then wipe his hands with a napkin. The early afternoon sun made his hair shine blonder than ever; he'd let it grow over the summer, and now an unruly lock kept falling on his forehead. He pushed it behind his ear, only for it to fall back after a second. His sunglasses were too dark to see his eyes, but his sexy smile more than compensated. It made Haley wish they were alone.

"What?" he asked, probably sensing her scrutiny.

"It's nice, you know? Being here and doing nothing with you. I missed that."

"I missed it, too. I'm sorry for the disappearing

act. I know I haven't been the most present boyfriend this summer, not even over the phone…"

"Stop." Haley leaned forward. "We already talked about it. Working with the best neurosurgeon in the country was too good an opportunity to pass. You don't have to feel guilty for going. Plus, it's all in the past now. Yeah, it's been a tough two months, but we're here now. Together. And we don't need to worry about being apart. We only have to enjoy each other."

"I plan to do a lot of enjoying," Scott joked.

Haley smirked. "You can start by helping me with the sunscreen." She fished a bottle of lotion out of her beach bag and handed it to him. "Or I might turn into a lobster." The skin on her shoulders was already starting to burn.

She hopped on Scott's towel and sat in front of him, facing away toward the ocean. Haley pulled her hair up to give him better access, shivering when the lotion landed cold on her back. The shuddering passed as soon as Scott's warm hands started kneading it into her skin, leaving Haley free to enjoy the gentle massage.

When Scott stopped, she asked, "Are you sure you got all the spots? UV protection is really important."

"UV protection, or getting a free massage?"

Haley tilted her head over her shoulder to look

at him. "Both."

"Great, since it's my turn now."

Haley turned completely, kneeling in front of him. "I love you," she whispered and leaned in to give him a soft peck on the lips. "I'm so happy you came back early."

"Me, too."

He hooked his hands on her hips and pulled her closer for a more thorough kiss. Mmm... if only summer could last a little longer...

***

Later that night, they stopped outside Scott's building to say goodbye.

"Don't go," he pleaded, holding her hands.

"I'm full of sand and I need a shower."

"You can shower here."

"But I don't have any clean clothes."

"So borrow something from me. You steal my clothes all the time, anyway."

Haley was about to give in when an ominous thought popped into her head. "Is David home?"

The other Williams brother had remained safely out of her mind all day, making her forget all about the hard conversation she needed to have with him, and the subsequent unavoidable hurt feelings. But now the sudden, real prospect of bumping into him was just too upsetting. Today had been perfect, and Haley wanted to remember it like that. No drama. No fights.

Scott gazed at the parking lot across the street. "His truck isn't here. He must be gone."

Well… if David wasn't at home…

"Okay," Haley agreed with a bright smile.

Inside Scott's house, they showered together and Haley borrowed one of his T-shirts to put on afterward. On her, it basically looked like a mini-dress. As underwear, she used a spare bikini and left her feet bare; no risk of catching a cold. They ordered a pepperoni pizza for dinner, watched a movie, and went to bed early, both tired after a long day at the beach. If she had to relive only one day for all of eternity, this would be the one she chose. As Haley fell asleep cuddled in Scott's arms, the notion that David had not yet come home briefly crossed her mind, only to be dismissed at once. Nothing had spoiled the best day of summer so far, and she wouldn't let anything ruin it now.

When she batted her eyes open next, daylight already filtered through the blinds. Her throat felt like dry earth left cracking under the sun. The pepperoni pizza had been super salty.

Without paying much attention to where she was or what she was wearing, Haley, still half asleep, lifted the arm Scott had wrapped over her chest and wriggled off the bed to go grab a glass of water.

She was heading for the fridge when a voice startled her.

"Good morning, Sunshine."

David's voice.

Clad in a dark suit, he sat at the kitchen bar eating cereal out of a bowl. His spoon-wielding hand was wrapped in white gauze and caught Haley's attention for a second before she lifted her gaze to meet his icy blue stare. He'd stopped eating and was eyeing her with an unreadable expression. Anger? Hurt? Scorn? All three?

Whatever emotion his face showed, the use of the wrong nickname hit Haley like a slap, jerking her fully awake at once. He hadn't called her Sunshine in months, and, okay, she'd already guessed he wouldn't be calling her Miss Robot anymore, not with Scott back, but she'd hoped they could've settled on a neutral 'Haley.'

Apparently not.

"David. Hi."

He gave her one last appraising look, then sneered. "I have to say… your taste in jewelry is much better than your taste in clothes."

Embarrassed by the comment, Haley lowered her gaze to the hem of the long T-shirt—*Scott's T-shirt*—she was wearing, which reached just above her knees. On reflex, she closed one hand around the pendant dangling from her neck. David's birthday present to her. Since he'd given it to her two weeks ago, she hadn't taken it off once.

"Don't be like that," she pleaded.

His eyes flashed. "Be like what? I merely criticized your fashion sense, or lack of thereof—"

"It's not that, David, and you know it. You're back to acting like a dick for no reason. We've gotten along all summer. Why can't you—"

"Things change," he interrupted.

"Nothing has changed. Scott is back, like you knew he would always be, and we're together. No news there."

"Sorry I'm ruining your reunion honeymoon with my bad mood."

"Stop the jerk act… This is not the real you."

"No? Why?" He dropped the bowl and spoon down on the counter and walked toward her. "Because I was nice to you a couple of times? Who said that wasn't the act? I'm only making it easier for you, *Sunshine*. Am I not?"

Such venom spilled from his words that tears welled in Haley's eyes. "Don't do this, David, don't be like this. I thought we could be friends?"

"Friends?" David let out a bitter, mocking laugh. "No, Haley, sorry… I can't be your friend."

"So what was this summer for you? A joke?"

"I'd call it more a mistake."

"Why?"

"I can't be in your life, not as a *friend*." David pointed at Scott's half-open door. "With him gone, I could pretend… hope… fool myself. But now… now, it's too damn hard."

"But David—"

"Why? Why would you even want to be my friend?"

"Because I care about you."

"Well, Haley, my feelings run a bit deeper, so you see how that might be a problem…"

"So you'd rather cut me off completely."

"Don't you understand?" Eyes flaring, he took another step toward her. "I can't see you with him. It kills me to know you're here, just one step away, but a whole universe apart. I don't want to hear your voice coming from under his door at night, or talk to you the next morning." He gave the T-shirt another seething glare. "Right now I can't even stand to look at you wearing his clothes… and I sure as hell don't want to be your friend."

Haley swallowed, lips trembling. "If that's how you feel. Do what's best for you."

"I will. I'm not the one with a problem admitting my real feelings."

Still glowering, David turned on his heel and marched out of the apartment, slamming the door shut behind him. Haley stood still, alone in the middle of the living room. She was breathing heavily, more shaken than she'd like to admit, and with a tightening in her chest that was hard to ignore.

It's better this way, her rational self tried to console her. *You can't have your cake and eat it, too.*

It wasn't fair to ask David to be her friend when he was in love with her. To stand by while she continued on her merry relationship with his brother. No, it wasn't fair. But the prospect of David being a stranger did nothing to lift Haley's mood.

And this mess was all his fault, anyway. He was the one having a sudden change of heart, after going above and beyond to become her friend over the summer. He had made her see his good, kind side, his devil-may-care personality… a taste of freedom. And now he couldn't just take it back. Nothing had changed; Scott had always been in the picture. David had always known… *even when we pretended it was just the two of us…*

With shaking hands, Haley grabbed a glass from the cabinet and filled it under the tap. The long, full gulps she swallowed did nothing to help her heartbeat slow down to normal. Seeing David so hurt had crushed her. Or maybe she was hurting, too, at the unwelcome awareness of having lost him for good.

Whatever the reason for the smoldering pain in

her chest, one thing was clear: yesterday's carefree mood was already a distant memory. It seemed like whenever she and Scott saw each other—no matter where, her house, his house, wherever—someone got hurt. And the constant guilt kept on wearing Haley down.

Before going back into Scott's room, she made a quick dash into the bathroom to splash a handful of cold water on her face, hoping to clear the clouds around her mind. But as she climbed back into bed next to her boyfriend, she was still unsettled. Thank goodness he still slept like a baby. If he'd heard even a snippet of her conversation with David…

How could I ever explain it to you?

As she lay in bed, staring at the ceiling and seeing only a pair of wounded blue eyes staring right back, Haley's phone vibrated on the nightstand. She picked it up, finding a series of texts from Alice.

Hey, where are you?

Are you coming home?

Madison and I are going to the mall to look for a new bikini later

For Saturday's party at Blake's house

(You and Scott are coming, right?)

Anyway...

We leave at 3

Haley stared at the screen for a few seconds. What better distraction than a trip to the mall and an afternoon of mind-numbing shopping with her best friends?

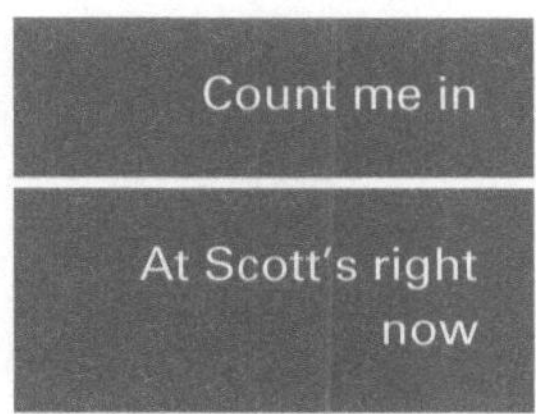

Will be home
before 3

She put the phone back on the bedside table and snuggled in closer to Scott. She kissed his cheek while he still slept, dropping her head on his chest afterward and closing her eyes.

Will it always be so hard?

Four

Haley

"Black or white?" Madison asked, holding up two identical bikinis, save for the color.

"Isn't the white one transparent?" Haley asked.

Madison stretched her hand inside the fabric to check if it was see-through. "Doesn't seem so."

"What about when it's wet?"

"Oh." Madison's face fell. "You're right."

She put both hangers back in place.

"How about a print?" Alice suggested, pulling out a gorgeous top. Asymmetrical, ruffled, with a trim made of mini pompoms. The fabric was in a pale pink shade with a budding flowers print.

"Wow." Madison's eyes widened; the boho-chic in her clearly couldn't resist. "This one's amazing. I'll try it on. Does it have a bottom, too?"

"Here." Alice handed her both pieces.

"You two pick one and join me in the fitting rooms. I want your opinion before I decide."

"Yes, boss," Alice joked. "You go ahead, we'll be right there."

Alice waited a while after Madison was gone before she spoke again. "See something you like?"

"I'm going with black," Haley stated.

"Like your mood?"

Haley's head snapped toward her friend.

"Yeah, it's that obvious," Alice confirmed. She took the top Haley had in her hands and switched it for another one. "If you have to go with black, at least try for an interesting shape."

The new top Alice had given her was a faux-wrap, cold-shoulder bikini top. Not exactly Haley's style, but what the hell. She already had a ton of plain, monochromatic black swimsuits, so if she had to spend the money she might as well mix things up a little.

"You make me live dangerously," Haley joked, selecting a pair of slips to match the top.

"And are you really making me ask?"

"Ask what?"

"The reason for the black mood."

Haley winced. "I saw David this morning. I walked into him coming out of Scott's room while wearing only one of his brother's T-shirts. He…"

"Was a douche?"

"He tried, but he really couldn't keep it up. In the end, I think he was just hurt."

Alice sighed. "At least now he can move on."

"Yeah, but it's never nice to cause someone pain."

"I know." Hands full of bikinis, Alice gave her a quick hug. Then, pulling back, she asked, "Nude or navy?"

Haley was glad Alice wasn't pressing the David topic; the less she thought about him, the better. She pointed to the nude halter bikini top with a high crochet neck. "When Jack sees you wearing that, he's going to pass out."

Alice put back the navy one and winked. "Perfect."

"What took you so long?" Madison complained, when they joined her in the fitting rooms.

She'd already changed into her swimsuit, and Haley honestly didn't get how her friend could be so insecure around guys. At five-foot-ten, not only was she statuesque, she simply was drop-dead gorgeous with her long, curly hair and big blue eyes.

"What do you think?" she asked, biting her lower lip.

"Buy," Alice said.

"Definitely buy," Haley confirmed.

Madison's entire face brightened up with a smile, the self-doubt gone. "Yeah, I love it, too. Let me see yours…"

***

They all ended up buying the pieces they'd tried on, and by Saturday morning Haley had to confess that some of her roommates' enthusiasm for this end-of-summer party had finally infected her. Everyone had been blabbing nonstop about how epic the party was going to be for weeks. The host, Blake Donovan, was on the basketball team with Jack and Scott, and had a huge house in the country—currently parents-free—with a massive pool and, apparently, could afford to throw an unforgettable party. Madison had proclaimed it'd be Gatsby-worthy, and even Alice had been talking about little else for the past few days. Haley didn't see what the big deal was; it sounded like any other house party, only fancier. But she was game to spend a day with her boyfriend and all their friends lounging by the pool, sipping cocktails—it was rumored Blake had hired a professional barman—and eating burgers right off the grill.

"Does Scott need a ride, too?" Madison asked. She was driving Haley, Alice, and Jack in her SUV.

"No, he's carpooling with David."

"So they're finally cool with each other?"

Haley shrugged. "Seems that way."

Haley actually had no idea if the brothers were cool. She hadn't asked Scott, and she sure as hell hadn't asked David. But from the way Scott had talked about his interactions with his brother since he'd gotten home, it sounded as if David hadn't been a bitch to him.

Oh, no. He's saving all his complaints for me.

Haley hoped Blake's house was big enough for her and David to be able to politely ignore each other. Just like old times… before he'd told her about their in-incognito kiss, before he'd forced her to like him, before he'd confessed he was in love with her.

Aaaaaaand… let's not think about that.

Clad in their brand-new bikinis and matching cover-ups, all three roommates walked out of their apartment to go meet Jack downstairs. It was only ten in the morning, but the party was supposed to last all day and maybe part of the night as well. So they'd timed it to get there early, but hopefully not first.

Twenty minutes later, Madison, following the car GPS, turned into a private alley and pulled up in front of an impressive building. A first look at Blake's country place confirmed that at least some of the buzz surrounding the party had been justified.

"I thought your country house was big," Alice said to Madison, mirroring Haley's awe at the size of Blake's house—*mansion, palace really.* "But compared to this, it looks like a studio flat."

"That's not *my* house," Madison said pointedly.

"Shall we go in?" Haley interrupted them.

"Yeah, let's go," Jack said.

The main door stood wide open—Blake wasn't that concerned with security, apparently—and they followed the instructions of a sign stuck to the door that read:

THIS WAY

Underneath, a giant arrow pointed to the French doors across the room. The entrance hall was mostly empty space, except for a corridor made of two rows of red-rope stanchions that forced them to follow a straight path ahead. To either side of the stanchions were an open kitchen with a huge island and a dining space on one side, and a modern, elegant living room on the other. It was easy to see why Blake would be worried about a bunch of drunk college kids wreaking havoc in here.

When they reached the French doors, there was another sign stuck on the glass.

IMPORTANT: CLOSE ME ONCE YOU'RE OUT!

They exited and did as instructed, closing the doors behind them, only to find another sign on the other side.

PARTY'S OUTSIDE. YOU DON'T NEED TO GET IN HERE.

THERE'S A BATHROOM BY THE POOL HOUSE

Oh, so there was a pool house, too?

To reach the actual pool, they had to walk down a flight of steps, pass an outside kitchen/dining area with a barbeque and two massive wrought iron tables complete with white sunshades, and cross a wide stretch of perfectly even green lawn. Behind the barbeque, a guy in a cook uniform was already busy setting up the grilling station.

They all walked down the stairs open-mouthed, admiring how the lower level of the garden opened on the Olympic-size swimming pool, attached Jacuzzi, cabana-style pool bar, and the pool house in the background. The whole pool area was surrounded by wooden chaise lounges with thick, plush padding, two roundish daybeds, and a row of white umbrellas.

Damn!

"I call dibs on the daybed," Haley yelled, running there.

She jumped in the center of the spacious

mattress and, turning around, she let herself fall on the mound of pillows that formed the backrest. Alice and Jack settled their things on a double chaise lounge on her left and Madison took a single one on her right. Now all that was missing was a cocktail in her hand and Scott by her side.

Still no sign of him. Haley checked her phone and promptly found a text.

> We're running
> late

> David had to drop
> by the office to
> turn in his last
> work assignment

> We'll be there in
> an hour or so

Whoa, investment banking really gave no one a break. Had David been up all night working? Haley wondered if she could've helped him speed up the process with her programming like she used to, or if they'd stuck him with one of those stupid analog projects. A pang of sadness tugged at her chest; she had no clue, and whatever David did was off-limits to her now. She'd only ever be able to get second-hand info from Scott on what was going on with his brother. But she had to get used to the idea they weren't friends anymore. They weren't anything at all.

Time for that drink.

As if on cue, Jack announced, "I'm going to the bar. What do you girls want?"

Madison straightened up in her chair and shaded her eyes to check out the bar. "Do you think the guy in the cabana is a real barman? He looks professional enough."

Everyone followed her gaze.

Jack shrugged. "I guess so."

"So he can mix up anything we want?"

"I can ask, but give me a back-up just in case."

"I'll take a Mai Tai, but only if they grind the ice. Otherwise, make it a vodka tonic," Madison said. Then, probably noticing that she'd just sounded a tiny bit "spoiled princess," she blushed and added, "Please?"

"No problem." Jack nodded and turned to Haley. "You?"

"A vodka martini, stirred not shaken, but only if they have olives. Otherwise…" She paused, pretending to think, but watching the dismayed expression on Jack's face, she quickly added, "Relax, I'm joking! Vodka whatever is good."

Jack smiled. "One blended Mai Tai, or vodka tonic; one vodka whatever; and you, babe?"

"Just a soda," Alice said. "I don't feel like drinking yet."

"Are you sure?" Jack asked, worried. "Are you okay?"

"Yeah, just pacing myself."

"All right, I'll be right back."

Haley waited for him to be out of earshot before asking. "Why aren't you drinking? Are you pregnant?"

"Oh my gosh, noooooooooo!" Alice shouted. "What the hell, Haley?"

"Sorry, but you've been blabbing about this party for too long to come here and not be drinking… What's up?"

"I got my period this morning, and the cramps were killing me, so I took a couple of painkillers. The instructions said not to drink alcohol while taking the pills, so I have to wait for a few hours."

"Oh, I'm sorry. Are you okay now?"

Alice flashed her a sly smile. "The drugs worked like a charm."

"Why didn't you tell Jack?" Madison asked.

"Because then he'd worry about me all day and ask me how I'm doing every five seconds, and I want him to have fun today."

"You're so sweet. Can I borrow you as my girlfriend?"

Alice blew Madison a kiss. "Sorry, I'm taken."

"Speaking of bad drinking habits," Haley said.

"We shouldn't drink on an empty stomach, and it smells like the grill is operational. I'm getting a burger. You guys want one?"

They both said yes.

"Bacon, cheese, BBQ sauce?"

Alice nodded, while Madison said, "No bacon for me, thanks."

Haley couldn't resist making a little fun of her friend. "Is any cheese okay, or should I ask for a specific one?"

Nonplussed, Madison answered, "I prefer Swiss, but any kind is fine, really."

Haley tried to keep a straight face but cracked when Alice started chuckling.

Madison stared at them. "Why? What did I say?"

"Nothing, Miss 'I'll Take a Mai Tai But Only If They Grind the Ice.'"

"But the Mai Tai sucks if the ice isn't blended."

"Sure it does." Haley rolled her eyes. "I'll be right back."

Haley could still hear Madison complain as she walked away.

"I'm not posh, am I?" her friend asked Alice.

"No, honey. But sometimes you do sound a bit high society."

Whatever Madison said back, Haley was too far away to hear.

Two burgers, one vodka whatever, and a Mai Tai—because it turned out they *did* grind the ice and the blended Mai Tai was really delicious—later, Scott finally arrived.

Even from a distance, he and David were hard to miss. True, there were plenty of tall dudes around since half the invitees were on the basketball team, but the Williams brother had that special magnetism about them. Standing there on top of the steps, searching the crowd with their eyes, they looked like the yin and yang of Haley's heart. Scott, with his summer-blond hair, dressed in a dark blue tank top and trunks, and David, in white head-to-toe with his mop of I've-just-rolled-out-of-bed midnight-black hair.

Haley stretched up on the mattress, waving her arms in the air for a few seconds before Scott spotted them and both the Williamses walked toward them. Haley watched David approach, trying to fathom how he'd behave today. He had dark shades on, and the part of his face that was visible—nose and mouth—gave nothing away. When he reached the daybed, he greeted them with a curt, "Ladies." Then he gave Jack a quick nod and turned on his heel, saying, "I need a drink."

So it was a "pretend Haley doesn't exist" kind of day. Whatever.

She decided to concentrate on the brother who

didn't come with a side of grouchy pie.

Haley shuffled onto the bed to make room for Scott and patted the mattress. "Come here."

He hopped on and pressed her against the pillows to give her the best "Hi, there" kiss, making all thoughts of David fly out of her head.

Pushing back, Scott smiled down at her. "What did I miss?"

"Not much. Just the best free cocktails and food of your life."

"Mmm, sounds like I have a lot of catching up to do. What are you all drinking?"

"Mai Tais," Haley explained. She was already tipsy. "Blended, not with the chunky ice."

Madison groaned from her chaise. "You'll never let me live that down, will you?"

"Sorry, no."

Scott frowned at Haley. "You prefer the ice cubes?"

"Oh, no. If it weren't for Madison here, I'd still be drinking sorry vodka whatevers."

"And how many did you have?" Scott asked, amused.

Haley took his hand and hopped off the bed, pulling him with her. "Come with me to the bar. It'll all make sense after you've had a few."

They didn't run into David at the cabana or back at their little corner of the garden. For a while, it seemed like the older Williams brother had disappeared into thin air. But as quickly as he'd vanished, David reappeared an hour later, only to keep his "ignore Haley at all costs" attitude live.

He sat on Madison's chaise. "Blondie," David said matter-of-factly. "We need to talk."

"Okay. Talk," Madison said.

"You're sadly out of a drink, and this conversation needs to be alcohol-supported. Can I offer you anything?"

"It's an open bar party."

"Well, in that case"—he stood up and offered her a hand—"let's go take advantage."

Only half-reluctantly, Madison took his hand and followed him toward the bar/cabana on the other side of the pool.

Haley made a conscious effort not to watch them, not to notice the way Madison seemed unable to keep a straight face at whatever David was saying. Weren't those two supposed to not be on talking terms? Whenever Haley saw them together, something stirred in the pit of her stomach. A snake of many coils: truths too hard to face, emotions too twisted to follow, and thoughts too dark to acknowledge.

Pretending not to look wasn't really helping; she needed to block David out of her life completely. She fished a bottle of sun lotion out of her bag and physically turned her back on

Madison and David, asking Scott to help her reapply the sunscreen. As Scott's hands massaged the tension out of her shoulders, Haley finally relaxed.

Five

Madison

Madison waited until they reached the other side of the pool to ask, "What do you want?"

"Hey, hold back on the hostility. I come in peace."

"Really?"

"I'd ask what's with the terrible mood…" David took a sip from his transparent plastic cup. "But I feel your pain, Blondie, quite literally."

A little smile forced itself on Madison's lips. "At least the brooding look suits you."

"Whoa, a compliment, Blondie? Careful there, I might think you're warming up to me again."

"Don't go getting a big head. I've only removed you from the undesirable number one spot."

"And who have I been replaced with?"

Involuntarily, Madison's eyes shifted toward Haley and Scott. They were talking as he massaged sunscreen on her back. Just as Madison looked over, Scott pressed a kiss to her friend's neck. Haley laughed and turned to kiss him full on the lips.

David followed her gaze. "Ah! The happy

couple. Revolting, I know. So I've asked you here because I have a proposition for you."

"Last time you propositioned me, it didn't end so well."

"Oh, come on, it wasn't all bad, was it?"

Madison scowled.

"Anyway, this one is a much more straightforward endeavor."

Madison cocked her head and relaxed her frown, shooting David a skeptical look she hoped would read as: *"I have reservations, but I'm listening."*

David caught the message. "I was thinking," he said. "Since we're partners in suffering, and we're at a party with plenty of free booze, what do you say we get absolutely trashed together?"

"I drove here."

"So did I, but Blake said I can crash in one of the guest rooms."

"Well, that solves *your* DUI problem."

"You can crash with me."

Madison crossed her arms over her chest and turned to study him. "David, what kind of game are you playing?"

"No game. I'm looking for a partner in crime. I'm not hitting on you, or proposing we do something unbecoming." He smiled wickedly. "I'm only asking if you'd like to drown your sorrows in alcohol with me. It's always sad to be a lonely drunk."

"And it's better to be a couple of drunks?"

David made a silly face. "Much, much better."

"And what about the others? We both had passengers."

"Blondie, let me tell you a secret…" He leaned in closer and whispered in her ear, "It's about time you did what's best for yourself."

Madison smiled. "You'd be a wonderful life coach, if only you weren't proposing I get shit-faced."

"Well, if you prefer to just stand here and enjoy the show…" David tilted his head in the general direction of Scott and Haley suggestively. Madison's eyes followed, and a quick glance was enough to make her stomach churn. "Be my guest."

David made to move away, but Madison grabbed him by the arm. "Wait!" If she had to endure the stomach sickness, she should at least have fun in the process. The others could find another ride home, or call an Uber. Or better yet, she'd lend them her car and return home with David the next day. Alice wasn't drinking, anyway. And Madison didn't have to babysit them. "I've changed my mind. I want to get drunk."

"Now we're talking." David smiled his signature lopsided smile and offered her his hand, asking, "What's your poison?"

Madison took his proffered hand. "Blended Mai Tai. They make the best ones here."

"Fine taste, Blondie…" David linked their arms together and steered her toward the pool bar. "You never cease to surprise me."

David ordered their drinks, and after passing Madison her Mai Tai, he raised his glass. "What should we toast to?"

"Why do you ask me?"

"You're the poet."

"Oh, so you've finally warmed up to the 'accursed and tormented soul' lifestyle?"

"Sometimes the heart leaves you no choice."

"All right," Madison said. Then she took a deep breath and put on a mock-serious expression. "It is the hour to be drunken!" she proclaimed in a solemn tone. "To escape being the martyred slaves of time, be ceaselessly drunk. On rum, on poetry, or on unrequited love, as you wish. But be drunk."

David looked at her, speechless for a second. "And you came up with that handy piece of depressing poetry on the spot?"

"No." Madison beamed at him. "It's Baudelaire—reinterpreted, of course."

"Well…" David bumped his cup into hers. "To whatever you just said."

He took a long sip and so did Madison,

relishing the cool taste. The danger with Mai Tais was that they went down so smoothly; the orange juice made them fresh, and the sugar disguised the rum all too well. Madison soon lost count of how many they'd ordered—but the barman sure seemed to be awfully familiar with them by now.

Halfway through their umpteenth Mai Tai and borrowed-from-dead-poets toasts, angry shouts distracted them from their drunken mission. Two dudes who looked even more wasted than they did appeared about to start a fight near the pool, just a few feet away from Haley and Scott's daybed. A tall, bulky guy with blond hair was arguing with another shorter, but equally bulky, brown-haired guy. Chests puffed out, brows set in menacing frowns, they yelled insults at each other. The blond guy was bare-chested, while the shorter guy wore a ridiculous Hawaiian shirt. Each guy had two or three dudes standing behind them, ready to intervene if the fight got serious. Madison didn't recognize any of them; there were far too many people at the party to know everyone.

Turning back to David, she asked, "Did you know Blake had so many D-bag friends?"

David shook his head. "I doubt half the people here are even his friends, but I don't care if a couple of losers want to beat the hell out of each other. We can just sit back and enjoy the show."

A loud crashing sound made Madison look

back to the scene. It appeared that Tall Guy had pushed Short Guy into a chair that had capsized, and now Short Guy was returning the favor. Tall Guy stumbled backward, losing his footing. As he flung his arms out in a desperate attempt to stay upright, he sent the entire contents of his glass spilling upward in a wide arc.

Unfortunately, the arc trajectory ended right on top of Haley. She let out a loud screech and jumped up from the lounger, wiping the sticky liquid from her body as well as she could with her hands.

In a matter of seconds, Scott was on his feet and marching purposefully toward the now full-fledged brawl—the friends of Short and Tall Guy had joined in the scuffle, pushing each other around and making everyone around them flee. Everyone except Scott, who was almost on them.

"Unless," David sighed, "my brother decides to play the hero and enters the melee, in which case…" He dropped his glass on the bar. "I have to help him defend the family's honor."

Haley was now trying to convince Scott to give up his quest, shouting at him to come back, that she only needed a quick shower. But Scott seemed deaf to her pleas. Of course, he would be the knight in shiny armor for the girl he loved.

Pity that's not me.

David seemed to have a less chivalrous

assessment of the situation. "What a fool," he said, pushing off the bar.

In the time it took David to walk from the cabana to the pool, Scott reached Tall Guy—who, tall as he might be, was still three or four inches shorter than either Williams brother.

The brawl was still roaring, but Not So Tall Guy had been pushed to the edges, and now he seemed more preoccupied with the newcomer towering over him.

"You spilled your drink on my girlfriend," Scott said, with such palpable fury that Not So Tall Guy was quick to go on the defensive.

"Yeah." David materialized by their side, taking a menacing stance next to Scott. "Kind of a dick move."

Outmatched two-to-one, Not So Tall Guy let go of his boldness rather quickly.

"Sorry, dude," he said to Scott. "I didn't mean to."

"You should apologize to her," Scott said, still visibly furious.

Not So Tall Guy wasted no time. He waved to Haley, yelling, "Sorry!"

"It's okay, I'm fine," Haley shouted back. "Scott, please come back here."

"See, it's all cool," Not So Tall Guy said.

David nodded to his brother and withdrew from the scene. Scott gave Not So Tall Guy one last withering stare, then started retracing his steps as well.

What happened next went down so fast that Madison took a couple of extra seconds to process it. One moment, Scott was peacefully walking back toward Haley. The next, he was falling into the pool, pushed inside like a human domino piece; two guys had careened into Not So Tall Guy, who, in turn, had fallen backward into Scott—back to back—propelling him into the water. But Scott was already at the edge of the pool and, before he plunged into the water, he hit the back of his head on the stone edge.

Haley's scream of terror shook Madison out of her momentary inertia. She dropped her glass and ran forward. David was much quicker to react. With an angered roar, he pushed everyone aside and, without removing his clothes, plunged head-first into the water, which was now tinged with blood, an ominous red nebula spreading from one corner to the rest of the pool. Scott's body lay unmoving at the bottom.

Haley

Haley didn't realize she was still screaming until Alice wrapped her arms around her and made her stop. They watched together as David disappeared underwater. He resurfaced in a few seconds, dragging Scott's inert body with him. Jack jumped over a lounger and joined them at the edge of the pool in an eye-blink.

"Call an ambulance," Jack screamed back at the girls.

Haley couldn't move. She couldn't do anything; she just stood there, trembling like a leaf, watching as Jack helped David drag Scott's body out of the water. Alice still had her wits about her and was quick to reach for her phone and call 911.

David and Jack laid Scott gently on the grass. He wasn't moving, and gave no sign he was alive. David bent his head sideways, putting his ear close to Scott's mouth, probably to check if his brother was breathing. The look of utter desperation on David's face as he straightened sent a chill down to Haley's core.

"Damn it!" David screamed, water from the pool mingling with tears streaming down his cheeks. "Don't you do this to me."

He pinched Scott's nose closed with one hand and began mouth-to-mouth resuscitation. He blew air into Scott's mouth four times and then, letting go of his nose, checked again for any sign of breathing.

"Come on, Scott, come on," David yelled.

Desperation mixed with sheer determination on David's face as he pinched Scott's nose closed again and started puffing air into him again. Halfway through the third breath, Scott's chest convulsed. David hastily helped his brother roll to the side as he vomited water. Once the spasm was over, Scott lay unconscious and deadly white. David bent his ear to Scott's mouth a third time and, this time, he straightened up with a crazed smile on his face.

"He's breathing. Someone call an ambulance!"

Jack threw Alice an interrogative stare, and she said, "We already did."

Everything happened in a blur next. The paramedics arrived quickly, and put an oxygen mask over Scott's mouth before moving him onto a stretcher and into the ambulance. David jumped in with them, and Haley watched them go, still too stunned to say or feel anything.

Her hands wouldn't stop trembling as she got changed into something clean, and she kept on shivering even though it was eighty degrees outside.

Alice, the only one of them who had had nothing to drink, drove them all to the hospital in Madison's car. They left the car in the parking garage and hurried toward the emergency room. Walking inside, Haley was assaulted by an unwelcome déjà vu. Unnatural neon light flashing past, careworn faces, and that typical hospital smell of disinfectant and despair. The same that had clung to her for days after visiting her father at Mercy Hospital in Buffalo. She'd almost lost him less than a month ago, and now she risked losing Scott as well.

No. Haley clenched her teeth with determination. *Scott will be fine.*

They found David pacing barefooted in the general waiting area. His clothes, a light white T-shirt and white board-shorts, left a trail of water droplets behind him and clung to his body like a second skin. He was a portrait of controlled fear: head bent low, gaze trained on the floor, and one hand rubbing his chin in a worried gesture.

"Man," Jack said, putting one hand on David's shoulder. "I've brought you a change of clothes." He produced a small bag Haley noticed for the first time.

David took the bag and stared at each of them in turn. When his blue eyes settled on Haley's, it was like staring into a mirror. Pale and weary, David looked as if he'd lost ten years of his life.

"Where's Scott?" Haley asked in a trembling voice.

"They're running a few tests on him."

"Did they tell you anything?" Alice asked.

David shook his head. "They wouldn't say much. Just asked me what happened, how he was revived, and then told me they needed to check his wound before they could tell me anything. He's getting an MRI…" David's jaw kept twitching as he spoke, and he wasn't able to stand still. "…or something." David smiled a bitter smile. "I'm afraid I've got no clue what that means. Scott's the neurosurgeon in the family. But they assured me giving him mouth-to-mouth was the right thing to do. Now we can only wait for the test results."

"Man, go put on some dry clothes," Jack insisted. "We'll be right here if anyone shows up."

David thanked him and disappeared into the closest restroom to get changed.

The girls sat on a couch nearby. Jack gave Alice a quick hug and then said, "I'm going to the hospital store to see if I can find a pair of shoes for David."

Alice kissed his cheek, and they all watched her boyfriend ask a nurse for directions and vanish down a side hall.

"Thank goodness for him," Alice said. "He's the only one who's thinking straight."

Haley nodded, making an effort to stop her lower lip from trembling. Seated in the middle between her friends, she lifted her hands, palms up, silently asking them to hold them. On her left, Alice's hand was warm and dry; on the right, Madison's was cold and clammy. Madison hadn't uttered a single word so far and, from the way she held on to Haley's hand, she must be just as shaken.

David came back from the bathroom wearing Jack's clothes and a deep frown. He stopped in front of them, looking like he was lost in thought.

"What's the matter?" Alice asked.

"I don't know if I should call my parents."

"They would want to know," Alice offered tentatively.

"Yeah, but my dad is in Hong Kong for work right now, and I don't want to scare my mom while she's home alone… But if it's something bad and I didn't call them…" David paused, visibly choked by emotions.

"How long before the doctors have the MRI results?"

"A couple of hours."

"You can wait to hear what they have to say and then alert your parents," Alice suggested. "That way you'll be able to give them better information."

"Yeah," David agreed. "It's not worth it to scare them." Then, looking straight at Haley, he added, "Scott will be all right."

Haley swallowed and nodded. She wanted to believe David, to share his positive attitude, but not until she spoke to Scott. Not until she saw his green eyes sparkle with life.

Six

Haley

"David Williams?" a young doctor called after a while.

Haley had no idea how much time had passed. It could have been minutes or hours.

"Yes, Doctor, I'm here." David stepped forward.

"If you could follow me, I'd like to give you an update on your brother."

David turned toward the group of people standing behind him. Besides Haley, Madison, Alice, and Jack, now all the guys from the team had joined them in the waiting room. With the school year about to begin, everyone had returned to Boston after summer break, and they'd all come to the hospital. Except for Blake, who had to deal with the police back at the country house since they'd opened an investigation into the accident.

"Please, Doctor," David said, "whatever you have to say, I will have to repeat it to them, and I'm afraid I'll do a very poor job."

"All right." The doctor sighed, clearly not pleased at having such a wide audience. "Your brother suffered a head injury. He needed stitches, but there's no skull fracture. However, the scans showed a small hematoma we hope will reabsorb on its own. We want to keep him here under observation for forty-eight hours at least."

"So, he's fine?"

"We'll only be able to give you a definitive answer once he wakes up. We've kept him sedated for now." Finally, the doctor smiled. "But, yes. Your brother should be out of the woods."

Haley let out a long exhale. She felt like she'd been holding her breath for the past few hours, and now she could breathe again.

"Can I see him?" David asked.

Haley got up to join him, but the doctor threw her an apologetic glance. "Sorry, it's only family at this point." Then, turning to David, he added, "Please come this way."

David returned half an hour later with a much more relaxed look on his face. "Scott's sleeping like a baby," he said, attempting a joke.

"When can other people visit him?" Haley asked.

"Sorry, they're not letting anyone who's not family in until tomorrow, or the day after. But you can have a peek through the glass. I'll show you to his room in a moment. Guys," David addressed all the people in the visitors' area. "Thank you all for coming, but you should go home now. There's no point in waiting here. I'll text you as soon as there's news."

The announcement was followed by a manly display of affection made of several back slaps, bro hugs, and hand-wrestler handshakes. Soon enough, all the guys had said goodbye and filed out of the hospital.

When everyone except Haley, Madison, Alice, and Jack had gone, David asked, "Did you guys bring Scott's phone?" He smiled regretfully. "Mine got toasted in the pool, and I still have to call my parents."

"Yeah." Jack, ever the cool-headed one, fished the phone out of another sack and handed it over.

David stepped away to have some privacy.

"You guys should go home," Haley told her friends.

"You're not coming?" Alice asked.

"No, I'm staying. Even if they won't let me into his room, I'd go crazy at home. I prefer to be here."

David came back a few minutes later, hands shoved in his pockets.

"How did it go?" Alice asked.

David puffed his cheeks, blowing out air. "As well as one could expect. My mom will come as soon as she can. She's calling my father now."

"I'm sorry, man." Jack put a hand on David's shoulder. "Can we help in any way?"

"No. Thank you, guys… for everything."

"We're going to go," Jack said, letting go of David's shoulder. "Call if you need anything."

David nodded and stared at Haley questioningly.

"I'm staying," she said.

After saying bye to everyone else, Haley followed David to Scott's room. Through the glass, Scott looked pale but serene, lying on the hospital bed with his back kept in a slightly raised position. He wasn't intubated but had an IV jutting out of his left arm and a gauze bandage around his head that resembled a white tennis player's headband.

Haley rested the tips of her fingers on the cold glass. "So the doctors said he'll be all right."

"He will," David whispered, standing right behind her. "He has to be."

"I got so afraid." Tears she'd been holding back all day finally rushed out. "There was blood everywhere," Haley sobbed. "If it wasn't for you, I... I don't know... I feel like I'm living my life in and out of a hospital. Everyone I care about is getting sick..." She was spinning down a dark rabbit hole of doom and gloom.

"No one is getting sick." David pulled her into a hug, and Haley's nostrils filled with the acrid smell of chlorine, David's usual scent of summer and the sea washed away by the pool water. "Scott had a dumb accident, but he's fine. And your dad is fine, too. We got scared today, that's all."

"Scott wouldn't be alive if it wasn't for you! The doctor said it, too. You saved his life."

"Hey." David let her go and grinned. "Don't sound so surprised."

"You care about him."

"He's my little brother."

"Yeah, but from the way you two act around each other… You always behave as if you hate him."

"We have a complicated relationship." David tilted his head, frowning slightly. "Usually there's a girl standing in the middle…"

Haley's heart skipped a beat.

"…But Scott is my family. I would never let something bad happen to him. On that note…" David took a step back. "I've been told it's good to talk to unconscious people, helps their brains"—David twirled a finger in the air near his temple—"mend, or stay active, or something. I'll go check if they have a book I can read to him at the hospital store. Can I leave you at the wheel?"

"Yeah, I'll call you if something happens."

"Right." David scratched the back of his head. "Remember to use Scott's number," he said, before jogging away.

He came back about twenty minutes later with a dark-covered paperback and an air of mischief about him. After looking around furtively, he said,

"All right, here's the plan. The doctors are making their rounds in half an hour and the nurses are changing shifts right now. I can cover you for five minutes."

"What do you mean?" Haley asked, surprised.

"As much as I'm sure my suave voice has extraordinary healing powers, I'm positive five minutes of hearing you talk to him will do much better for Scott's brain than anything else. Come on." He opened Scott's door. "I'll knock when it's time to come out."

Haley gave him a grateful smile and snuck into the room. With David's words fresh in her ears, Haley started talking at once, doing her best to keep her tone even as she spoke to her unconscious boyfriend.

"You gave us all a scare today, you know? But my honor is intact, at least." She laughed softly. "But next time, please try to ignore the drunken hotheads, yeah? I wouldn't be able to survive something like today twice. I… I was so scared. The moment I saw you fall into the pool, my heart stopped. Scott, the blood was everywhere. I was sure you had none left in you. I thought… Well, I guess I didn't think much at that moment. I sort of lost it."

Haley took Scott's hand. It was cold and dry. "You should've seen David. He went berserk… I've never seen him so… so… *emotional.* Your brother loves you, you know, even if he sometimes makes it so hard to see, he really does. He snuck me in to let me talk to you, even if for only five minutes—"

A sharp knock interrupted Haley's speech.

"And now I have to go before the nurses discover me and kick me out." Haley leaned down to stamp a kiss on Scott's forehead, the part still free from bandages. "See you tomorrow. I'll be just outside."

After opening the door only a crack, Haley poked her head out. David beckoned her to come out and shut the door behind her. No one was around; they'd gotten away with it.

"Are you going to be all right out here alone?" David asked.

"Yeah. Maybe I'll go get a book myself." Haley lied, she didn't have the focus to read right now—but David didn't need to worry about her on top of everything else. She tilted her head toward the paperback in David's hands. "What did you buy?"

David turned the book in his hands. "A thriller. It's supposed to be good." He shrugged and shifted back and forward on his toes before saying, "I'd better get going. Knock if you need something."

Haley gave him a curt nod and went to sit in the empty row of chairs in the small atrium in front of Scott's hallway. Wrapped in eerie silence, the Neurology wing of the hospital offered little to do other than stare at the wall and think. Haley shifted her butt to find a comfortable position, then let her emotions run wild.

Her mind flew to Scott at once, to the months they'd spent apart, and to the few days they had had together since he came back… and, especially, to the hole that had appeared in her chest when she'd seen him lying unconscious on the lawn while David tried to revive him.

David.

He was everything and the opposite of everything: good-hearted and cruel, kind and scornful. He had so many layers Haley doubted she'd ever be able to peel them all off and find the real David, or if it was even a wise aspiration to have.

After a long time sitting, Haley lay down and shifted her blank staring from the wall to the ceiling, her brain still buzzing with questions. As her lids started to droop with exhaustion, one final, ominous thought crossed Haley's mind. She fell asleep wondering if it was possible to be in love with two people at the same time.

***

Haley woke up the next morning with her face resting on a small white pillow and her body under the cover of a hospital blanket.

And where did you two come from?

The answer came to her lips almost immediately. "David."

She straightened up, groaning at the pain in her sore back. Pillow and blanket or not, hospital chairs were most definitely not a comfortable bed. Stretching her neck left and right, Haley stood up, wrapping the blanket around her like a poncho. She peeked into Scott's room through the glass; nothing had changed from the night before. Scott slept while his brother read to him. David's voice didn't carry out of the room, but it was funny to watch the little expressions he made as he narrated the story. A small frown here, a surprised face there. He grimaced and then pouted in an "aha" sort of way, completely absorbed in the story. And even if Haley couldn't hear a word of what he said, she had a clear sense of where the book was going, or when the hero faced a trial or scored a point.

"Hey," someone close by said, making her jump.

Haley turned to find Madison standing in the hall next to her.

"Hi." Haley greeted her friend with a hug. "What are you doing here?"

"We couldn't sit still back at the house."

"We?"

"Jack and Alice came with me. They stopped at the cafeteria to get coffees for everyone. Are there any developments?"

"No. The doctors will take him off medications later in the day. We can only wait."

"How are you?"

Haley wrapped herself tighter in the blanket. "I'm holding in there." She turned her gaze once more to the inside of the room.

Madison imitated her. "Is David reading to Scott?"

Haley nodded. "Yeah, he said something about keeping Scott's brain stimulated while he's unconscious."

"What's the book?"

"A thriller. Something with a famous actor on the cover. I can't remember the name."

Madison narrowed her eyes at the paperback and scoffed. "Leave it to David to torture Scott with mass-market fiction even on his sick bed," she said jokingly, speaking like a true book snob.

Haley studied her friend. "I know you're not a fan of David's, but—"

"David's all right," Madison interrupted.

Haley coughed in shock. "Even after what he did to you?"

Madison hesitated, staring at the floor and

chewing on her lower lip.

"What is it?" Haley asked.

"He apologized to me a while ago."

"When? Why didn't you tell me?"

"He asked me not to…"

Haley frowned questioningly.

"When he apologized, I had just spotted you two together at the library, so I accused him of having an agenda; of apologizing only because he hoped I'd report to you so that he'd score points. That's when he made me promise not to tell you, to convince me the apology was about me and not you."

"You still could've told me."

"I wasn't sure the gesture wasn't a reverse psychology trick, and I wasn't convinced he had no angle."

"And you are now?"

"Yes, I believe he was sincere. David can be horrible, but he's also good sometimes."

Nailed it, Haley thought, then added aloud, "That's why you've been talking to him again."

"Uh-huh."

Haley would have asked more, but they were interrupted by Alice and Jack bringing the coffees. Soon after that, a procession of nurses and doctors began when the time to wake Scott up arrived.

The young doctor from the day before closed the blinds. As before, David was the only one admitted into the room. He came out what seemed like an eternity later with a big smile on his face.

"Someone would like to see you," he told Haley.

The last lump of worry Haley didn't realize she still had in her throat vaporized, and she hurried inside. Scott was sitting on the bed, his back resting on a mound of pillows. He was pale and had bluish circles under his eyes, but he was smiling… even more when he spotted her.

"How are you?" she asked, approaching.

"I'm… still recovering from the realization that I've become a sorry, college frat boy cliché."

"Oh, so you're playing the 'let's-joke-about-it' angle?"

Scott smirked. "Too soon?"

His green eyes sparkled and his smile was sexier than ever. He winked, and Haley knew everything was going to be fine.

Seven

Madison

Will I see him today?

First-day-of-school jitters mixed with unrequited-love anxiety as Madison walked into the Baker Center building, the facility where a lot of Humanities classes took place. The first course of the fall term was a creative writing workshop Scott should be attending, head injury permitting. She hadn't seen him since the previous week at the hospital. After two days in observation, Scott had been discharged with the doctors' recommendation that he be kept under constant supervision for at least a week. So Haley and David had taken turns playing nurse, meaning Madison had seen little of her roommate since release day.

Haley had temporarily moved in with Scott, and her visits home had been quick and targeted. She'd come to grab a change of clothes, drop off her dirty laundry, and not much else. When asked about Scott's recovery, she'd say he was doing fine and everything was okay. Answers not nearly satisfying enough for Madison.

She tried not to resent Haley; at least, not more

than usual. That first night after the accident had been hard. When everybody had gone home, Madison had wanted to stay. Even if visitors for Scott were still forbidden, she'd wanted to wait outside his room to be close to him, just like Haley had done. But Madison didn't have that right because she wasn't his girlfriend, and asking to stay would've been too weird for everyone. An implied reminder of an awkward truth everybody knew and nobody wanted to discuss.

Well, except for David, maybe. He was always game for a self-pitying chat about the "happy couple." Madison half-scoffed, half-smiled.

Anyway, Scott didn't know about Madison's feelings for him—at least, she hoped he didn't. But she could trust Haley with her secret; she'd never tell him, even if Scott was her boyfriend. And neither would his brother. So explaining to Scott why she'd felt the need to camp outside his hospital room for a whole night would've been *inconvenient,* to say the least.

Catching a glimpse of herself in the hall's windows, Madison checked out her reflection, hoping the extra care she'd put into her makeup and outfit that morning wouldn't be too evident. Satisfied with what she saw, Madison stepped into the classroom with an inhale of anticipation, her heart beating a little faster than usual. But a quick scan of the intimate space revealed Scott hadn't arrived yet.

The classroom was super small. Teachers liked to keep workshops limited, and this one was no exception, with only twelve students admitted. An oval, wooden table occupied most of the space and, around it, half of the thirteen chairs were already taken.

With a sigh, Madison took a seat with an empty chair on either side. Scott could be late; there was still time for him to walk in and sit next to her. Four students had yet to arrive, which gave Madison a fifty-fifty chance of spending the next three hours sitting beside Scott. Those odds reduced drastically when Clare Montgomery came in a few minutes later and sat on Madison's left.

Still one free spot, Madison thought, throwing a hopeful glance at the empty doorway.

With little to do before the professor arrived, and not wanting to stare at the door like a hawk, Madison busied herself organizing her notepad and pens on the table. At five minutes to one, a towering shadow appeared in her peripheral vision, making more than one head turn—female heads. Madison followed their gazes to the threshold, dismissing the newcomer with a quick glance.

Two seconds later, she did a not-so-subtle double take. It was Scott, wearing a longish military green shirt and faded jeans, looking unbelievably gorgeous with a new half-shaved, half-long undercut hairstyle so different from his usual that Madison hadn't recognized him at first.

"Scott." She jumped up from her chair. "You made it."

"Hey." Scott smiled, and the whole room seemed to brighten.

"How are you?"

"Great…" He gave her a quick hug and took the chair next to her, earning Madison a few eye-daggers from her fellow female students. "…all things considering."

"What's up with the hair?" Madison asked.

Scott turned his head to show her his nape, passing his hand on the lower, buzz-cut half. "I felt ridiculous going around with a huge bald patch in the back of my head, so I shaved half off." A large adhesive bandage was still plastered on the spot where he'd hit the pool rim. Turning back toward her, he added, "I still have to get used to it."

Well, me, too. The top of Scott's hair now fell on his forehead, seeming much longer than it had before, and the style really suited him.

"Why? You look great," Madison blabbed. She instantly regretted the spontaneous comment and tried to rein in the furious blush that threatened to make an unwelcome appearance whenever she was this close to Scott.

"Haley likes it, too. But it's good to have a second opinion." Scott winked.

Madison's stomach flipped, and she scrambled to find a different subject other than how good Scott looked. "So you've recovered from having to listen to a thriller feast for a whole night?" she joked, feeling one hundred percent like the book snob she was.

"David is a pretty good narrator, actually."

"Still, I would've picked a Jack London novel if I had to read to you for twelve hours straight."

Scott turned his gaze on her and studied her for a second. "He's my favorite author. How did you know?"

Madison's face heated up, a*gain.*

Good job, Madison, she chided herself. *Reveal your little stalking habits, won't you?*

"Oh, really? London is one of my favorites, too," Madison lied.

"Really?" Scott's face brightened up at once. "Which one of his books do you prefer?"

Madison was struggling to find something to say—she had read *The Call of the Wild* for another course and remembered doing an allegory study on *White Fang,* but that was as far as her Jack London knowledge went—when the professor came in, greeting all of them with a severe, "Good morning, class," that snuffed out all conversation.

Ding-dong, saved by the proverbial bell.

Phew.

And it's only the first day, Madison cursed inside her head. *How am I going to last a whole year?*

I have to be strong and pull through, she repeated to herself. *Be strong and pull through.*

The school year couldn't have started in a worse way, and now she had to actually read all of Jack London's novels back to back—and preferably before the next class she'd share with Scott.

Georgiana

Georgiana felt strangely self-conscious walking the familiar halls of Caspersen Student Center with her bump clearly showing for the first time since she'd gotten pregnant. At the end of the spring term her stomach had still been smooth and flat, but over the summer a giant bubble had popped out of her midsection and, at twenty-two weeks pregnant, no amount of color blocking or smart dressing could disguise her giant belly.

Eyes followed her as she strode toward her class, trying to project her usual confidence. The indiscreet stares didn't really bother her;

Georgiana was used to making heads turn. Over the years, she'd grown accustomed to the extra attention; basked in it, really. Rich, beautiful, and the daughter of one of the most powerful and recognized lawyers in Boston, usually people wanted one of two things when they looked at her: to date her, or to be her.

But not today. Guys were throwing surprised side-glances at her stretched-out belly, and then, horror-struck in a glad-it's-not-me way, they'd stare at Tyler walking beside her. But what rattled Georgiana the most was how girls showed the same attitude. Instead of envying her, they seemed to pity her.

Um, hello? I'm married to the most gorgeous guy in our year, what's with the pity-party?

For the first time since getting married, Georgiana realized that not everyone dreamed of having a husband and a family, at least not as early in life as Georgiana would have both. Yeah, right. These were career-hungry women. The halls of Harvard Law School probably weren't the best focus group for proud stay-at-home-mom wannabes. Not that Georgiana was ever going to be a stay-at-home anything.

Still, Georgiana was relieved when what had felt very much like a walk of shame ended. Unfortunately, things did not improve once inside the classroom.

For one, Rose was there. The bane of Georgiana's existence, not only was she Tyler's best friend, but also Ethan's girlfriend. They were the two most important men in Georgiana's life, her husband and her brother, and Rose had her claws sunk deep in both. And if that wasn't already enough, today her nemesis looked too attractive for her own good in her prim class uniform—dark jeans, light-blue V-neck sweater with a white shirt underneath, blue blazer, and women's derby shoes. Plus, and what irked Georgiana the most, Rose was thin like a stick.

And for two, the sneers in here were far worse than outside. It didn't take Georgiana long to catch her fellow female students staring at her belly in groups of two or three, and then gossiping among themselves in hushed tones with their heads bent together. Again, not a single envious face among them, only derision and pity.

Georgiana let Tyler slide into the middle seat and took the outer seat of the row—with the baby pushing on her bladder, she had to go to the restroom so often that letting Tyler sit next to Rose was a strategic necessity. Gosh, these seats were uncomfortable. Her bump barely fit under the narrow table that spanned the entire row of chairs. Georgiana soon realized she wouldn't be able to bend forward and take notes. Oh, hell. Never one to give up, Georgiana placed her tablet on the table and opened the new dictation app she'd bought foreseeing this eventuality.

A sudden burst of laughter made her snap her neck up. She swept the room with a burning, ice-cold stare until her eyes came to rest on a group of three girls who used to hang on Georgiana's every word. Now they giggled among themselves while purposely not looking at her.

Let's see how much you're going to laugh when your ovaries are all dried up and you're still spinsters living with their ten cats like lonely, crazy cat ladies, Georgiana thought bitterly.

The school year couldn't have started in a worse way. And now she had to pee, *again!*

Haley

Last first day of school ever, Haley thought, with the same melancholy she remembered from her first day of senior year in high school. Only this time, graduation was the real thing. There wouldn't be a new school the following year; only work, and the beginning of a different phase of life. Job applications and adult responsibilities were concepts scary enough for Haley to almost second guess her decision of not applying to grad school. But the one thing she wasn't going to need for sure in this new, grown-up life was more debt. No need to be scared of the future, anyway. Different didn't necessarily have to mean worse.

Right.

Still, she couldn't avoid looking at the buildings, the halls, and the familiar faces of her fellow Computer Science students with a bit of ruefulness as she walked into her first class of the day.

The professors, however, didn't seem to share any of her nostalgic musings. Her schedule was pretty packed already, and each of her instructors opened their lectures with a right-off-the-bat, we-don't-want-to-waste-any-time teaching approach, which didn't leave Haley much time to romanticize over the past and the future as she was barely able to keep up with the present.

So much so that the end of the last lecture of the day came almost as a surprise. All melancholy lost and glad the day was over, when Haley walked outside the main SEAS building, the sun warmed her skin, and the air still smelled like summer.

Smiling, she fished her phone out of her bag.

Scott picked up on the second ring. "Hi, babe."

"Hey, how's my favorite patient?"

"Tired."

"You didn't overdo it today, did you? The doctors said you should take it slow."

"I did, I promise… Just had a long day."

"Yeah, me, too. Where are you now?"

"Crossing Harvard Yard as we speak. You?"

"I was heading toward your place, but I'm too tired to cook. What do you say we grab a bite together?"

"Perfect, also because I suspect we left an empty fridge at home."

"It was David's turn to go grocery shopping."

"And I'm sure he'll go, but I'm hungry now and who knows when he'll be back."

"Yeah, I'm starving, too. Meet me at the bookstore?"

"Perfect."

"I'll get to you in five."

***

If the day could've been described as one of the last of summer when they entered Pinocchio's to grab a square-cut slice of pizza, the weather had definitely switched to "Hello, fall" when they walked out.

"Oh, it's raining!" Haley shouted, opening the restaurant's door to get out.

She made to run under the downpour, but Scott grabbed her waist and pulled her close to him— her back to his chest—under the shelter of the restaurant ledge. "Come here, silly," he murmured. "You'll get all wet."

Haley struggled to breathe, trapped in his grip. No, not trapped… only *torn*. Splintered in two. One part of her wanted to be exactly where she was: warm and dry, safely wrapped in Scott's arms. Secure, protected. But there was another part of her that wanted to run free in the rain, to be wild, spontaneous, and who cared if she got wet…

"It's only water…" a familiar voice whispered inside her head.

Haley tried to stop the thought before it took shape in her mind, but she was too late. Already an image of David standing under a summer storm and beckoning her to join him had invaded her thoughts, clear as day.

His dark, wet hair plastered to his forehead as he caught her wrists and held her hands close to his chest. The intense look in his eyes as he leaned his head down. The phantom of his lips on her forehead after he'd kissed her. A whispered promise: *"The next time we kiss, you'll want to just as much as I do now…"*

And then, his rage. *"You're a liar, Haley. You're lying to me, and you're lying to Scott, and most of all you're lying to yourself."*

And the dark emotions in his eyes as he'd made another promise.

"I won't go away, Haley. I'll always be here for you." David's words echoed inside her head

with the same intensity as if he were saying them to her now. *"I love you."*

Haley leaned back against Scott, gripping his arms more firmly. No, she definitely couldn't think about that day… not now… not ever…

Eight
Alice

On the first day of school, Alice woke up with a start long before the alarm clock was scheduled to go off. On impulse, before even fully opening her eyes, she grabbed her phone and checked her texts. Jack had disappeared on her the day before, and she'd gone to bed worried. It wasn't like him not to reply to her messages or at least to reach out to wish her a good night.

As soon as she touched the screen, a multiple text notification appeared. Alice sighed in relief and opened the chat. Unfortunately, the unlocked phone revealed two clipped, not so comforting, possibly I-don't-love-you-anymore speech bubbles:

No 'good night,' no kiss, no 'I love you.' Alice scrolled up to her part of the chat.

I DON'T WANT TO BE FRIENDS

Hey, you

Where have you been all day?

Excited about school tomorrow?

I could've used another week vacation

Want to grab a coffee before class?

Jack, are you there?

Guess not

I'm going to bed

Night

:*

She honestly didn't see where she'd gone wrong with her texts. Okay, she'd asked him where he was twice, but only because he hadn't hit her back. That couldn't be labeled as oppressive or clingy, right? So what was up with him? Was he already getting tired of her? No, *impossible.* This was the old, insecure Alice talking. Jack's Ice was confident her boyfriend loved her. So why was Jack being such a—*Okay, let's stop right there... Keep calm and don't insult the boyfriend. You're going to see him in a few hours and everything will be fine.*

I hope you're right, Alice concluded her mental rant with herself.

After a quick breakfast and a gigantic cup of coffee, she put extra care in choosing her outfit and doing her hair and makeup, feeling half-silly, half-cute. After all, Jack had now seen her in every possible state: dressed up, down, not at all, with spot-on makeup, with morning-after panda eyes. Maybe he hadn't seen seriously hangover Ice yet, but that was it.

Ready and pampered, Alice walked to the Science Center, enjoying the still warm sunrays of late August. Along the department hall, she passed a boy and a girl—clearly freshmen, from the way they stared around themselves, disoriented—and shook her head with fondness. She remembered another couple of freshmen three years ago, who'd stood with their heads bent close over a map, trying to figure out where the hell they were supposed to go on their first day of school.

Not needing to look at a map anymore, and alone, Alice navigated the corridors and stairs of the building with the casualness and confidence reserved for senior students. The first lesson of the day was a large one, and so it took place in one of those movie-theater type classrooms: rectangular—longer than it was wide—with sloped floors and rows of chairs with attached mini-desks on each level.

Alice poked her head inside to check if Jack had already arrived. For Chemistry major students, this was the auditorium where most of the large classes took place, and they had a favorite spot: the first and second chairs in the center, next to the stairs, three rows back from the front. No one was sitting there yet, so Alice quickly hopped down the steps to grab the two seats. She sat in the one farther away from the stairs, placing a notebook on the other one to save it for Jack.

Once settled with her desk up and notepad ready to take notes, Alice turned toward the back of the room to search for her missing boyfriend.

Nothing. She pulled her phone out of her bag—five to nine, and still no sign of Jack.

Alice was about to send him another text asking where he was, when a quick succession of flashbacks passed through her mind. They all involved Jack complaining about girls who "kept texting him and didn't get the message" while he tried to ghost them. Most of his breakups had consisted of him simply disappearing until the poor girl eventually *did* get the message.

Am I that girl now?

A lump of dread clogged Alice's throat, and she had to swallow. With clammy hands, she grabbed her water bottle and sipped a few gulps to calm herself. Not that it worked very well. Especially since the professor—Mr. Harrison, a new guy—had just walked down the stairs and Jack was still MIA.

It wasn't like Jack to be late. Had something happened to him? Horrible accident scenarios started playing in her head. But then she remembered that Jack *had* replied to her texts. No matter how short, unsatisfying, and unloving his reply had been. So her boyfriend probably wasn't lying in a hospital somewhere. That was something, at least.

He could still be at the gym. The basketball team had an informal meeting scheduled that morning. That fresh intel came from Haley—

whose boyfriend had *not* gone incommunicado—but the meeting was supposed to be only a pep talk, and it should've ended well before their 9 a.m. class started.

Whatever Jack's reason for being missing, texting him now that Harrison had arrived wasn't an option anymore. With the advent of social media and other distracting apps, smartphones had officially become teachers' number one public enemy. All professors seemed to lose their bearings at the mere sight of one in the hands of a student in their classes. So, not wanting to destroy her participation score on the very first lecture, Alice promptly stashed the offending piece of smart tech away.

All throughout the lesson, however, she sneaked glances behind her shoulders whenever Harrison was busy writing on the blackboard. Eventually, on her eighth or ninth try, she spotted Jack sitting in the last row, his face half-hidden in the shadows. He was looking straight ahead and gave no sign of having seen her.

She kept looking at him for as long as she dared, but she had to turn back to the front of the room without having met his eye. This made no sense. Why was Jack sitting back there? Well, he could've arrived so late that he hadn't wanted to attract too much attention toward himself by walking down the stairs.

But usually, whenever Jack was late for class—which happened a lot once regular practice with the team started, and he had to run to lectures straight from the gym—he'd wait for whatever professor to turn around and jump into the chair she'd saved for him at the first good occasion.

Not today, it seemed.

For the next hour and a half, Alice wasn't able to concentrate on the lesson. Not a word of what Harrison said filtered through her mental noise. By the end of class, she had no idea how they were going to be graded, how many midterms they'd have, when—*if*—there was going to be a group project, if the groups would be decided by the students or assigned, and when the first homework was due. Not to mention the actual content of the lecture. The board was filled with molecular structures, and Alice had no clue what they were supposed to do.

For the entire morning, there'd only been one recurring thought drilling a hole through her brain. Jack was mad at her. He was clearly avoiding her... putting distance between them. Why? *Why? Why? Why?* The question kept pushing on her skull from the inside-out and left no space for anything else.

Familiar with Jack's avoidance techniques, Alice shot out of her seat the second Harrison dismissed them and ran up the stairs, barely managing to catch up with him as he walked out of the class.

She grabbed him by the elbow. "Hey."

Jack turned toward her and didn't smile. "Hi."

Alice came close to kiss him, but he pulled free of her grip, saying, "Not here. It's not professional."

Professional? They'd been working together at a pharmaceutical company all summer, and Jack had had no problems kissing her in the hallways. And this was only school. True, it was their first day of class as boyfriend and girlfriend, and they hadn't discussed an on-campus PDA policy... but... Jack had never refused to kiss her. Except... that day at the library, when she'd first tried to kiss him and he'd turned her down without room for interpretation.

Alice forced the déjà vu away and vowed to keep calm and try not to kill her boyfriend. "Why didn't you come sit next to me?" she asked in a neutral tone.

"I was late. I didn't want to come down to the front row with the professor looking."

"That never stopped you before."

"I knew the teachers. Harrison is new."

It all sounded so reasonable, so plausible, and also so much *bogus*. Alice couldn't shake the feeling Jack was lying to her. She was about to call him out on it when he spoke again.

"Let's go, we're going to be late for our next class."

Seething inside, she followed him along the hall to their next lesson—a lab this time. Even though they shared a station, the situation didn't improve one bit. Jack didn't look at her once and didn't speak a word the entire time unless it was related to the experiment they were conducting. And by now, Alice was so mad she was fine with not talking to him. She took it out on the lab equipment instead, handling the various alembics and test tubes with far less care than they deserved.

If Jack wanted to be an asshole, he could be her guest. She would be an asshole right back. But, *just maybe,* he wasn't the wisest to be such a jerk to his girlfriend when, with a few, well-mixed chemicals, she could cook up an explosive and torch him to the ground. Especially not when she had all the ingredients all nicely lined up in front of her.

Steady, Alice. Keep calm and do not torch your boyfriend.

When the lab was over, Alice decided to keep her mouth shut and see what Jack would do. They had no more classes for the day, so she was curious to see what his next excuse would be. She didn't have to wait long.

As soon as they stepped out of the building,

Jack said, "I have to go meet Coach Morrison."

"Didn't the team meet already this morning?"

Jack shrugged. "He asked me to meet him again for lunch."

"Okay, see you later?"

"Yeah, sure. I gotta go now." He took a step backward, as if to make it clear she wasn't getting a goodbye kiss. Not that she wanted one. Right now, all Alice wanted to give Jack was a goodbye punch. "I'll see you around."

"You'll see me around?" Her nostrils flared. "Jack, what's up? You've been weird since last night—"

"I don't have time to do this right now." He jogged another couple of steps back, and added, "I've got to go."

Jack turned on his heel and sprinted away.

On the way home, Alice had to fight back tears. When she got home, she stormed inside, so angry she even scared Blue, her pet bunny, when she banged the door to her room shut. What now? Being the first day of school, she didn't have much to do. No papers to write, no studying, no reading… nothing. She was free to stare at the ceiling and keep asking herself what she'd missed. She tried to read a book—something Madison had insisted she read—but of course not a single printed word filtered through the Jack haze.

Eventually, the four walls of her bedroom

made her so claustrophobic that she moved into the slightly more spacious living room. And that's where Haley found her when she came home much later: sitting on the couch, staring into space, nibbling at her fingertips.

"Hey," Haley said, frowning at her. "What have you done to your nails?"

"They were collateral."

Haley's frown deepened. "For what? Are you alone? Is Madison home?"

"She put her 'go away, I'm reading' sign on the door, so she must be in there."

"What's up with you?"

"Jack is mad at me." Alice dropped her elbows on her knees, bouncing them up and down in a nervous gesture as she kept staring into space, waiting for an answer to appear out of thin air. "And I've no idea why."

"Could it have to do with the article?"

Alice's head snapped up, and she focused on her roommate, who was now occupying the armchair in front of her. "What article?"

"The one about Peter. He gave an interview to the *Chicago Sun-Times*, and they've re-posted the piece on the team's website. You haven't seen it?"

"No. I don't regularly check the Crimson's website."

"Hey, don't shoot the messenger. Scott told me about the interview; I just got back from dinner with him."

"No, sorry, I'm not mad at you. Is Scott doing okay?"

Haley mmm-hmmed yes, so Alice continued, "I've been going crazy since last night. First Jack disappeared, and then today he's been…" Alice took a breath. "…*not very nice*. You think it has to do with this interview?"

Haley shrugged. "Scott said Jack was as much fun as assembling IKEA furniture at the team meeting this morning."

Oh. *Ooooh!*

"Do you have a link to the article?"

"Wait." Haley took her tablet out of her bag, unlocked it, tapped multiple times, and handed it to Alice. "The good stuff is at the bottom."

Alice paused a second on Peter's picture. Well, there was no denying it: he looked dashing, smiling at the camera in his red Chicago Bulls uniform, muscular shoulders peeking out of the tank top and bright blue eyes piercing the screen. She skim-read the first part of the article and scrolled to the near end as Haley had suggested, stopping when she caught the words *broken hearts*. She backed up a little and started reading.

> "So, Peter, did you leave any broken hearts back in Boston?"

"Only mine."

"A bad relationship?"

"Actually, a perfect one."

"And what happened?"

"My girl told me our lives were about to change. I guess she wasn't much into the long-distance scenario."

"I'm so sorry to hear that. Whoever that girl is, she surely let go of a wonderful man. But good news for all our single ladies here in Chicago..."

Alice stopped reading. She returned the tablet to Haley and grabbed her phone to text Jack with a vengeance.

Alice stared intently at the screen, registering the moment Jack received the text and the instant the chat app signaled he had read it. She kept her gaze so laser-focused it might've burned through the glass. Soon after Jack had read the text, the three little dots signaling he was typing a reply appeared and disappeared several times before an actual reply came in. It was a short:

Maybe

Relief washed over her.

You have no reason to worry

You know that, right?

No, I don't

He made it sound like you broke his heart or something

You said you
never were that
serious

That you never
loved him

And I didn't

Peter must've
been
exaggerating for
the press

He's probably
going to use his
alleged broken
heart as a pickup
line

You know how he
is

Did you tell him
we are together?

No

I haven't kept in touch

(which should make you happy)

It does

Have *you* told him?

He used to be your best friend

Used to

When did it stop?

When he started dating you

Worst seven
months of my life

Alice smiled before typing:

You're jealous

And you're cute

I'm not cute

And I'm not
joking

Having to watch
you with him

Every day...

You can't
understand

I can

No, you really
can't

Alice scoffed. The nerve of him! She started typing a list of names, careful to leave Madison's out of it, to make him see just how much she got it.

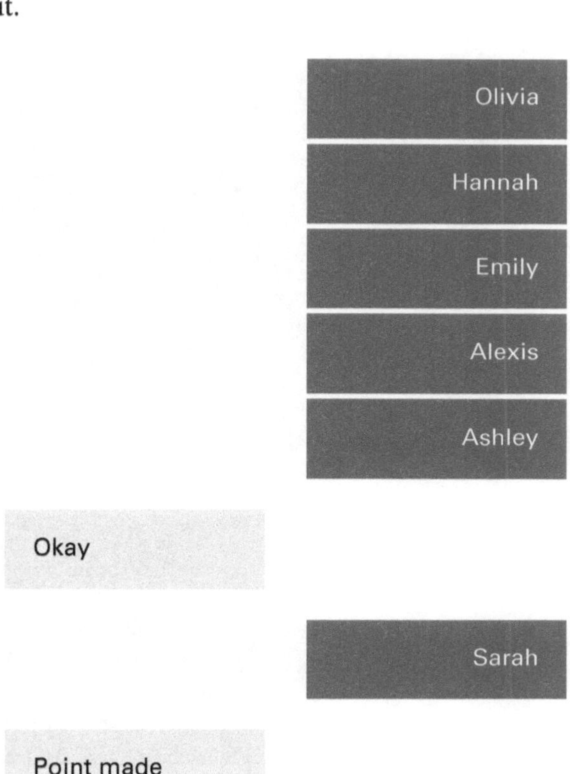

Okay

Point made

Elizabeth

Samantha

I get it

Alyssa

Taylor

Jennifer

Jessica

You can stop now

Julia

Emma

Kayla

I DON'T WANT TO BE FRIENDS

Megan

Nicole

How do you even
remember all of
them?

Lori

Becky

Because each and
every one of
them was a stab
through my heart

Now *you're* cute

I'm not cute

Can I come over?

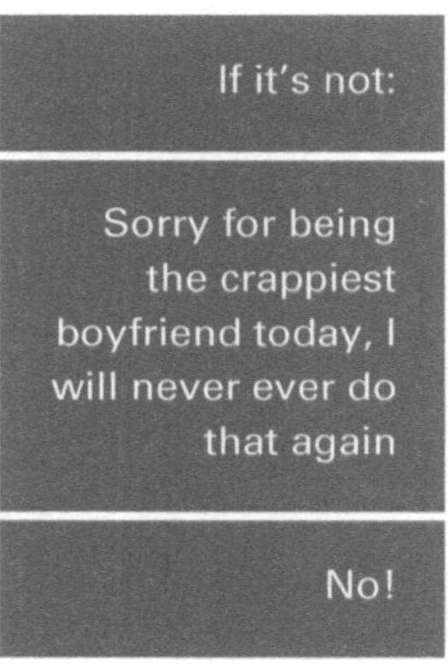

When he knocked on her door half an hour later, Alice's instincts were torn between kissing him and slapping him. She went for the kiss first, and then she not-so-lightly punched him in the chest.

"Don't you ever scare me like that ever again. Deal?"

He flashed her that boyish-but-roguish smile she loved so much. "Deal."

She hugged him and kept her face buried in his neck for such a long time that, at one point, Haley shouted, "Get a room!"

Alice lifted her head and whispered, "That's not such a bad idea."

She pulled Jack backward into her room, pushed him onto her bed, and kicked the door shut behind her. Straddling him, she said, "So, how much groveling are you prepared to do?"

"All the groveling you require."

"Good. And you have to tutor me as well. I didn't get a word of what Harrison said this morning."

Jack smiled a mischievous smile. "I can work with the student-teacher scenario."

"Uh-oh," Alice scoffed. "I don't think so. It's going to take a while before you get some, Mr. Sullivan."

He pouted and made a cute face he knew she couldn't resist.

"I'm serious." She tried to keep a straight face and failed miserably. "So what was it you wanted to tell me?"

Jack beamed at her. "The coach asked me to be

team captain!"

Alice let out a loud squeal and collapsed on Jack, hugging him and kissing him. "That's fantastic. Amazing! Did you expect it?"

Jack's face turned serious. "I think it was between me and Scott, and with the injury so fresh, I suspect the coach didn't want to put too much pressure on him."

"I'm sure you would've gotten it anyway. You're going to be a wonderful captain!"

Jack placed his hands on her hips, his thumbs massaging her sides while he stared up at her, gaze intense. "I'm sorry for today, I really am. I behaved like shit, but when I read the article… Peter is still a sore point for me…"

"I know, but next time just *talk* to me. I don't care if you want to yell at me or tell me to go to hell. If you're mad, let it out. We can't solve anything if I don't know what's going on inside this pretty head of yours." She poked him on the forehead. "Deal?"

"Deal."

"Now you can tell me you love me and start with all that groveling, yes?"

Dead serious, Jack said, "I love you." Then he flipped her on the bed, so that now he was on top, and started kissing her neck. "And I know exactly the kind of groveling you need…"

Nine

Haley

After a first week of school made of free evenings, the basketball team came knocking on Scott's door pronto on week two. Scott had not yet been cleared by the doctors to play basketball. They wanted to monitor him for another couple of weeks and do another scan before they permitted any intense physical exertion. But Coach Morrison insisted that he attend all of the team's practice sessions anyway—to familiarize himself with the new team members, the new playing schemes, and, more generally, to keep him in the loop.

Since the basketball team had kidnapped Scott, Haley was spending Thursday night at home, doing nothing. She was sitting on the couch living vicariously through the lives of her 237 Facebook friends. The distraction earned her more than one reproachful look from Madison, who insisted time spent on social media was a total waste, and why didn't she read a good book instead? *Reading is good for mental health, it improves memory, reduces stress, boosts brain function, blah, blah, blah...*

Her roommate was probably onto something, but right now all Haley wanted was a bit of not-so-stimulating Facebook snooping into the lives people wanted her to believe they led, with a side of the occasional my-life-sucks, self-pitying post.

At least, that had been the plan. The danger in navigating the Facebook waters was that all kinds of friend-*ships* could sail by. In this case, a certain other Williams brother she hadn't heard from in a while appeared out-of-the-blue on her feed.

Haley stared at David's post, frowning.

David Williams is
feeling naughty
at Monroe C.
Gutman Library

That was weird. David never checked in on Facebook. Was it a coincidence he'd shared his location tonight? Did he know Scott would be at practice?

Haley didn't care if it was a plot; they hadn't talked about their friendship since that horrible first morning after Scott had come back from California, and she needed to get a few things out. She checked the time of the post... only ten minutes ago.

She jumped up from the couch and, after feeding Madison a lame I-forgot-I-had-a-project-meeting excuse, she grabbed her coat and bag from the hall and was out of the apartment in a blur.

At the library, she searched the café and study room, but there was no sign of David anywhere. She circled back, trying some of the smaller rooms, but still nada. She went back to the main room and settled at a table, ready to admit defeat. After lying to Madison about having a group project meeting, Haley couldn't walk back home only twenty minutes after leaving. So she took her laptop out of her bag and resigned herself to a dull hour of killing time on the internet. Until…

Haley's phone flashed with a new text message… from David.

Are you stalking
me?

Haley jumped in her seat, turning her head left and right, but he was nowhere to be seen.

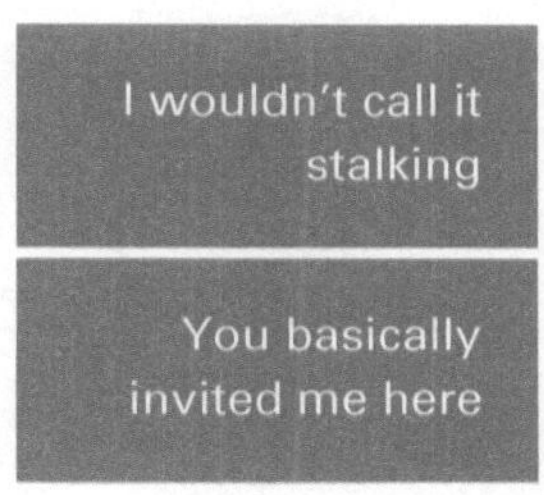

Really, how?

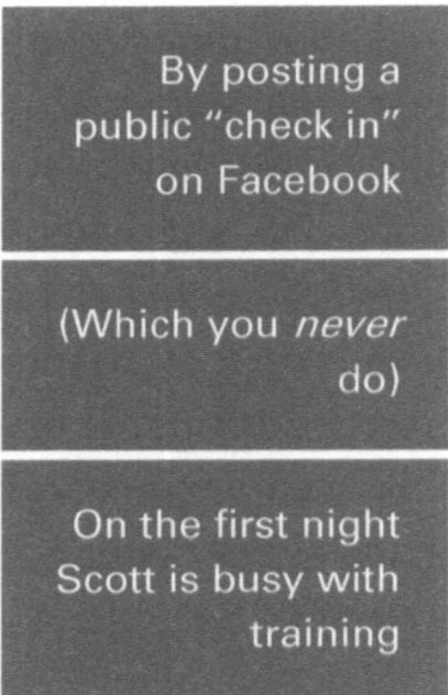

You check my
profile often?

Haley shook her head. He was being impossible like always. And it was driving her crazy to be blind when he clearly had eyes on her.

Stop looking for
me

You won't find
me unless I want
you to

He was so damn infuriating!

Why are you
here?

Because I miss you, was Haley's first instinctive response. But no way would she type that. She bought a few seconds by rolling the phone in her hands. What to write?

Stop trying to
come up with a
politically correct
answer

Just tell the truth

Coming here was
a mistake

Haley made to pack her things and go when, out of nowhere, David materialized in front of her and took the chair on the opposite side of the table.

Blue eyes flaring, he asked, "Why are you here?"

"Because I missed your company, all right? Happy?"

The corner of his mouth curled up into that infuriating-but-oh-so-sexy lopsided grin. "You really couldn't bring yourself to say you've missed *me*."

Haley glared.

"Fine, all right." David threw up his hands with a little shrug. "I'll take what I can get. So what's been going on with you lately?"

"Madison told me you apologized to her," Haley blurted out.

She'd been dying to tell him she knew forever.

"Glad to know I can trust Blondie with a secret."

"Why did you ask her not to tell me?"

David shrugged with his eyebrows. "The apology wasn't about you."

"Why do you make it so hard for people to see the good in you?"

"Because I'm not a *good* guy. Not all the time, at least. I am good and I am bad and I'm all the shades in between, and I don't want to have to live up to anyone's expectations. You're already dating the right brother if you want a Good Samaritan, or the one who pretends to be."

"Now you're being snarky again."

"Snarky? Me? I'm only telling things how they are. We all have our flaws. But the thing that makes me just go crazy is that because my brother projects being a goody-two-shoes, everyone assumes he's perfect. Scott wants so much to be the good guy he'd never admit he'd done anything awful even if he has."

"We're not talking about Brigitte again, are we?"

"Well, it's the perfect example. Scott goes behind my back, steals my girlfriend, and somehow I'm the bad guy."

"You can't judge him on a single thing that happened ages ago. Besides Brigitte, when has he ever hurt anyone?"

"That's a big besides."

"No, it's not. And stop making this about Scott—"

"Let's make it about us, then," David cut her off. "Why are you here, really? Are you tired of living the righteous life? Are you looking to live dangerously? Why come all the way here just to see me? Don't tell me it's because we're friends. Is that really all I am to you?"

No. You're the stranger who stole my heart with a summer kiss, you're the friend who drove me seven hours in the middle of the night just to get me home in time, the boy who made me run under the rain, the man who apologized to Madison and asked her not to say anything. The answer popped into Haley's mind, unbidden. *You're the person who makes me question everything.*

And you're Scott's brother.

With that last thought, Haley's already ragged breath worsened. "I can't be here."

Before she could get up, David grabbed her hands from across the table, his blue eyes flashing. "You can run away now, but you can't outrun your feelings."

"I'm in love with Scott."

David stared her dead in the eye. "Are you saying that to convince me, or to convince yourself?"

Heart beating so fast in her chest it might break out, Haley fought back the tears. There was a vortex of emotions wreaking havoc in her, shattering everything it found in its path. And Haley feared that if she stayed here a second longer, there'd be nothing left behind.

"David, let me go," she pleaded.

He did so without a word, his eyes burning ice as they tore into hers. Haley couldn't hold that gaze; she was too weak. So she fled the room, feeling the lingering touch of David's stare on her long after she'd walked out of the library.

Away. She had to stay away from him.

Ten

Haley

In no time at all, the relaxed mood of the first weeks of school vaporized, and all Harvard students found themselves swept into the middle of the fall term with homework accumulating, massive studying to be done, and midterms looming over them. And in just over a week, the basketball season would officially kick off.

Scott would be busier than ever. Haley still couldn't fathom why anyone would *voluntarily* submit to the pressure and the schedule-nightmare strain of playing on a college varsity team. But Scott loved the game, and so did Jack—Alice was as puzzled—and so had David, and Peter, and everyone else on the team. So there must be something to it the "girls" weren't grasping.

But before the no-drinking, not-a-weekend-without-a-game-until-March season started, the players—as per Coach Morrison's concession—still had their last free-pass-for-all night: Halloween. This year the thirty-first would be on a Monday, so all the parties around campus had been scheduled for the preceding Saturday—a.k.a. today.

As was tradition, the basketball team would go with a group costume. This year they'd picked Minions costumes—ironic, since the shortest guy on the team was six-foot-two. They'd been Smurfs the previous year. Haley chuckled at the thought. How much had changed that night. Alice had gone out to make Jack jealous and had ended up dating Peter instead. Hence the Christmas Hawaiian trip, and Haley's meet-cute with Scott—*and the not-so-cute introduction to unmasked David.*

Last year, Haley had been single at Halloween. Her heart had still been harboring an irrational hope—a gut-twisting hope that squeezed the breath out of her whenever she caught sight of a black feather—of running into a certain masked stranger...

And let's not go there.

After their unofficial meet-up at the library, David had disappeared. No more subtle Facebook invitations, no texts, no nothing. Haley hadn't seen him on campus, and at his and Scott's house, he was a ghost, always coming in late and dashing out before anyone was awake. If Haley got thirsty in the middle of the night, she'd learned to deal with the urgency and wait until she'd heard the front door open and shut before going out to fetch a drink.

It was hard to believe it was Halloween

already. It had only been a year ago she didn't—*exactly,* kisses under the stars didn't count—know either Williams brother. It all seemed like ages before.

"I'm not sure about this," Madison said, bringing Haley back to the present.

All three roommates were in Madison's room, doing their official "dress rehearsal" for the night. After much debate and not many choices available—it had taken them forever to decide on costumes, and all the good ones had already disappeared off the racks—they'd settled on being chipmunks. Haley was Alvin in a red sweatshirt, black leggings, and long, pulled up red socks, Madison was Simon, with blue socks and sweatshirt, and Alice was Theodore in green.

"We're basically dressed for the gym," Madison insisted.

"We can still add the initials," Alice offered, standing in front of the mirror next to Madison and holding a big, cut-out "S" made of white adhesive paper close to her chest.

"Then we'll be dressed for the gym and lame," Madison said. "I still think we should've gone like handmaids."

Madison had wanted to go dressed as characters from *The Handmaid's Tale* by Margaret Atwood.

"And how is the red-nuns look any better?"

Haley said. "I like this costume. It's easy, comfortable, and we can wear sneakers."

"But it's so simple," Madison protested. "Do you think people will get it?"

"If we put on the initials," Alice insisted. She grabbed Madison by the shoulders and spun her around. "We can stick them on the back." She held the "S" near the middle of Madison's back.

Madison turned her head over her shoulder to stare in the mirror. "They're not so lame like that."

"And we can all draw whiskers on our faces and get hair-bands with ears," Haley said. Madison was warming up to the chipmunks idea, and they needed to strike whilst the iron was hot.

"I still have my cat ears from last year," Alice said.

Madison turned to face her, affronted. "We're chipmunks, not cats."

"I'm sure they'll have chipmunk ears at the store," Haley mediated, trying not to laugh at Alice's dismayed face. Madison was definitely taking this costume thing a bit too seriously.

After several trips to different costume stores—because, no, they couldn't use mice ears; they were too black, too big, and too round—one YouTube makeup tutorial on how to draw the perfect rodent nose and whiskers on one's face, and much hair curling, they were finally ready.

The party house was the same as last year, a

six-room, double-story townhome that had a ground floor large enough to host such a big party. It wasn't a "one party every weekend" situation; the guys living there only threw a few big parties every year, and Halloween was hands-down their best. They put the extra care in decorating the house, garden, and back patio with pumpkins, spiders in their webs, skeletons, and such.

Thanks to their sneakers, Madison, Haley, and Alice had an easy time walking the few blocks to get to the party house. And thanks to their sweatshirts, they didn't need to risk bringing a coat and losing it, or having it ruined by party hazards. They'd walked last year, too, but without heels, it was a much quicker, less painful business.

Halfway to the destination, they bumped into a horde of Minions. In head-to-toe yellow and with an average height well above six feet, they were easy to spot. Less easy was for Haley and Alice to identify their respective boyfriends. When they did, they couldn't help but laugh. Scott and Jack were silly adorable in their yellow onesies with big, round, fake eye goggles on top of their heads.

Scott kissed her and frowned at her sweatshirt. "What are you supposed to be?"

Madison pushed past them, muttering, "Told you no one was going to get it."

"We're *The Chipmunks,*" Haley explained, and she turned around to point at the big "A" on her back. "I'm Alvin, Madison is Simon, and Alice is Theodore."

"Oh, I get it now. Shouldn't you girls be speaking in shrill little voices?"

Haley obliged him, trying to make a good impression of that I-just-inhaled-helium-from-a-balloon little voice. "I can talk like this all night if you want."

"Nope, just kidding. Your usual voice will do just fine." He offered her his elbow. "Shall we?"

Chipmunks and Minions made their way to the house together and, since there were so many of them, they had to queue at the entrance and enter in smaller groups of two or three. Haley was impatient to get in, but just a few minutes after reaching the back of the living room, the main party area, the walls were pressing in on her.

The atmosphere inside the house was suffocating in comparison to the crisp air outside. With the party already in full swing, throngs of boys and girls were drinking, sweating, and dancing body-to-body to the hard beats of the loud music blasting from a set of giant speakers positioned on either side of the fireplace. It wasn't just the volume of the music that felt oppressive; whoever was in charge of the playlist had gone full horror on them, and was spinning one dark, violent tune after the other.

Also, the lights were all off, the only

illumination coming from a thousand fake candles scattered all over and a few fairy lights strung over doorways and around the fireplace. Still, the scarce light produced long and gloomy shadows on the walls, made even spookier by the great number of party-goers clad in blood-splattered, grotesque costumes who had taken Halloween too literally. Not to mention the many hooded figures hovering around.

Haley shivered despite the heat. Oh, please, she was being silly. It was Halloween. Costumes were supposed to be gruesome, and as for the stale air, they just needed to open a window or two. She tackled the closest one, relishing the fresh intake of cool air. But she couldn't spend the night breathing out of a window, so she beckoned Scott to follow her out of the living room and into the somewhat less crazy kitchen area. A cool beer was what she needed.

Haley almost chugged the whole cup in one sip, and refilled from the keg, needing more.

What's wrong with me?

Something about tonight didn't sit right with her. Same as in horror movies when the innocent sorority girl doesn't realize the killer is watching her, and she's about to die.

Mmm, hello? No one's going to murder you. I promise, Haley's inner self chided.

Yeah right, no need to stress.

Haley took another sip of beer and followed Scott back into the living room. She searched the walls for another window to open… and froze.

Deep in the shadows, passing behind the dancing crowd, a mask caught her eye. Black and full-faced, with only holes for the eyes and a triangular opening at the bottom for the mouth and chin. The mask looked as expensive as Haley remembered it, with its silver beading, black feathers, and a surface so smooth it appeared to be made of the finest porcelain.

When Haley's eyes met with the blue ones peering out of the black mask, the throbbing beat of blood in her body sped up. Her throat clenched, making absorbing the scarce oxygen in the room all the more difficult. The temperature inside seemed to grow even warmer, making it impossible for Haley to breathe. Or move at all. She was only able to stare into David's eyes as he approached the patio doors, moving behind the mass of sweaty party-goers swaying in rhythm with the music—vampire girls dancing sexily with each other, witches grinding against their zombie partners, and all kinds of monsters throwing their hands in the air.

The black tux costume bestowed on David an eerie glamour, like a modern-day vampire prince, making the boy behind the mask even more handsomely wicked. Stopping by the French windows, he fixed the feathered and jeweled mask on his face and bowed his head in a barely perceptible nod.

Palpitations, followed by sweaty palms and a light head, were Haley's first response to the sight of David wearing *the* mask. The unexpected appearance of a ghost from her past was too much. She was reacting in ways she didn't like, but couldn't ignore. He had power over her; Haley could no longer deny it. But she could choose not to act on it.

Feeling as guilty as if she'd done something wrong, she stared up at Scott. He seemed unaware that his brother had joined the party. He just stood there peacefully sipping his beer and nodding his head in time with the awful music.

Haley stared back at David. He was now leaning against the wall next to the patio doors, regarding her with a satisfied little smirk that seemed to say, *"The ball's in your park."*

"Hey, Scott." Matt's voice made her turn again. "I need a teammate for beer pong. You in?"

Scott looked down at her. "Do you mind?"

"No, not at all. Go ahead."

The timing was perfect. While Scott played, she could go discreetly kill his brother. With all the fake blood around, no one would notice. Tonight, she could get away with murder.

"You're not coming to cheer?" Scott asked her.

"No, actually, I need a breath of fresh air."

Scott kissed her and followed Matt toward the beer pong table in the farthest corner of the room opposite to the patio doors. *How convenient.* Haley waited until they were a few throws into the game and completely absorbed by it, before marching toward David.

"What the hell?" she said without preamble, shoving him against the wall with both hands.

"Whoa-oh, calm down." He smirked under the mask. "I like it feisty, but I have my limits. Should we pick a safe word first?"

"David, cut the crap!" she yelled, part out of frustration and part to be heard over the deafening music. "You disappear for two months and then you show up like this?"

"Like what?" he asked, infuriatingly calm.

"Wearing the same mask you had on the night we met."

"Oh, you mean this little trinket." He readjusted the elastic behind his head. "This was expensive. It's good economy to wear it more than once."

"Why here? Why tonight?"

"It's Halloween, in case you haven't noticed. Masks are all the rage."

He was being impossible, and the music, the heat, the artificial fog...

"I need some air," Haley said. She slid the

patio door open and walked out. "Do not follow me," she ordered, slamming the door in his face.

Not two steps out, and she heard the door slid open again. Without turning, Haley walked to the railing and gripped it with both hands. Soon someone was standing right behind her.

"Why shouldn't I follow you?" David whispered, his mouth close to her ear, so that Haley could feel his breath blow softly down her neck.

"I'm in love with your brother," she said, sounding rather desperate.

"So you are," David said—angry, merciless.

Haley wriggled sideways and turned around to face him. *Bad move.* He was the exact replica of the boy she'd fallen in love with that night at the masquerade. Because he was the boy of the masquerade. Only now he was so much more.

Her head spun with memories from the summer ball. The flirting, the dancing, and David kissing her. The touch of his lips on hers, his arms wrapping around her body—

No. No. No. A walk down memory lane wasn't a wise choice. Right now she needed to get out of this conversation and go find Scott.

"You can't keep doing this," she said, in what she hoped was a composed, rational voice. "You keep going hot and cold on me. First we're friends, then we're not, and then you pull a stunt like this. What do you want?"

"*I* keep going hot and cold?" he hissed. "I don't think so. I only came to a Halloween party wearing a mask—"

"Stop lying!" Haley yelled.

"You stop lying!" David shouted back. He took a step forward, grabbing her by the shoulders. Eyes locked on hers, he hissed, "What do *you* want?"

He was too close, and Haley's chest heaved. She was dangerously close to tears, and the few beers she'd had were enough to make her too damn emotional to answer that question.

"Is everything all right here?" Scott's voice interrupted.

Haley's eyes snapped to him, hoping darkness and the whiskers painted on her face would help conceal how upset she was.

"Yeah," she said, trying to master a normal tone and shrugging free of David. "I was just going to come look for you. Did you win the game?"

Scott didn't appear convinced, even less so when David spun around and greeted him. "Hello, brother. Nice gear," he said, eyeing the Minion costume sarcastically.

"David."

Scott seemed confused. After the accident at the pool, and the way David had taken care of him in the following weeks, he wasn't so quick to get angry with his brother. But now Scott was staring between his girlfriend and his brother with a deep, worried frown.

"I didn't know you were coming," he finally said.

David shrugged. "Oh, you know. This is the only half-decent party near campus. I'd better get back inside before all the pretty girls are taken." He sent a pointed look Haley's way.

She watched him move back inside and braced herself for the inevitable questions, but Scott only asked, "Are you sure you're okay?"

"Yeah, it's just so stuffy inside."

"Not anymore. They've opened all the windows. I was coming to open the patio door as well when I saw you out here... The situation seemed *tense*."

"Not really, just—"

"There you are." Madison barged through the now-open doors, interrupting her. "I've been looking for you everywhere. We're playing girls versus boys. You have to come now or we'll lose the table."

Haley shrugged and looked up at Scott, "Do you mind?"

"No." He forced a smile, clearly not happy their conversation had to stop. "Who's on the boys' team?" he asked Madison.

"You, Jack, and Matt. Come on, you two, hurry up." Madison beckoned them inside and, without waiting to check if they were following her, she pushed her way back toward the beer pong table.

Haley plastered a smile on her face. "Come on, she'll kill us if we don't get there in two seconds."

Scott stared at her for a moment longer, his expression seemingly saying, *"This conversation isn't over."*

She nodded in acknowledgment and went back into the house where, with all the windows open, the air was breathable again and not faint-inducing. Eager to have an excuse to drink more and not have to explain the whole David-in-the-black-mask situation to Scott, Haley joined Alice and Madison at their end of the table, yelling, "Ladies throw first!"

Eleven

Haley

"You're upset," Scott said—a statement, not a question.

Ah, so he hasn't forgotten, Haley thought ruefully.

They'd been walking in silence toward her house for a good ten minutes now, and after an entire night of drinking and partying with no mention of the David Factor, Haley had hoped Scott had dropped the topic for good.

Apparently not.

"I'm not upset," Haley said, keeping her eyes on the concrete.

"Okay, but you were before when you were talking to David. Why?"

Different brother, same annoying questions.

"It was nothing, Scott, let it go."

Scott stopped, but Haley pretended not to notice and kept walking to see if he'd follow her. He didn't, so she had no other choice than to stop and turn to face him. "You really want to do this now, at two in the morning, while we're freezing our asses off in the middle of the street?"

"I don't know, Haley," he said, his features so

serious that not even the Minion costume could infuse humor into the situation. "What is it we're doing?"

"Discussing your brother, *again*."

"Well, there'd be no need to discuss my brother *again* if I hadn't found you talking to him with the face of someone whose cat just died. And don't tell me it was nothing because I'm not an idiot."

"It was that stupid mask, okay? Are you happy now?"

"What mask? What's wrong with the mask?"

Haley stared at the ground. "It was the same one he was wearing the night we met."

"And by *the night you met*," Scott said in such a tense, cold, un-Scott voice that Haley had to look up at him. He was speaking through clenched teeth, his jaw tense. "What you really meant *is the night you kissed him*."

"What do you want me to say? I can't cancel the past."

"I'm not worried about the past."

"What's that supposed to mean?"

"Look at you. My brother shows up wearing a stupid mask, and you get upset, then pretend nothing has happened all night—nice act, by the way—and finally, when I ask you about it, you try to bullshit me."

"I wasn't bullshitting you, I just thought it

wasn't important."

"Do you often get so upset about unimportant stuff?"

"Why do you have to make such a big deal about it? David came to the party wearing that mask to provoke me, and it worked. You know how he is; he's the master at pushing a person's buttons."

"No, Haley, he's a master at pushing *your* buttons. Can you stop pretending for a second?"

"Pretending to do what?"

Scott studied her for a long moment. "The only thing I can't tell is if you're just lying to me, or also to yourself…"

Different brother, *definitely* same annoying questions.

"Lying about WHAT?" Haley shouted back.

Scott stared at her dead in the eye, and when he spoke next he did so in a tone so calm it bordered on vicious. "Do you have feelings for my brother?"

Haley wanted to say 'no,' to shout it. But somehow her throat seemed to have clogged up and her mouth didn't open. Eyes wide, she could only stare at Scott, unable to speak. They stood like that for an eternity, looking at each other while an unconfessable truth was being shared between them.

Scott's jaw tightened, and he broke eye contact

first. Gaze now fixed on the curb, he said, "Let's go. I'm walking you home."

Haley fell into step next to him, not sure what to say, her heart beating as fast as if she'd been running. In the end, she could only come up with a lame, "I'm sorry."

It came out strangled, and it didn't convey nearly a tenth of what Haley was feeling.

"It's my fault," Scott said. "I went away, and that's all he needed to weasel his way into your life."

"Scott, it's not your fault. Whatever David has over me, it doesn't matter. Scott, stop." She placed herself squarely in his path and grabbed him by the shoulders. "I'm in love with you. I chose you, and I choose you every day."

He gently but firmly shook her off. "See, Haley, the thing is: it shouldn't have to be a choice. Least of all one you have to make every day."

"What are you saying?"

"Honestly? I don't know. Maybe you were right. We shouldn't be having this conversation at two in the morning."

They walked in silence the rest of the way to her house. In front of her building, she climbed up a step so that their eyes were level, and asked him if he wanted to come up.

"Not tonight," he said. "I think I'm just going

to walk home and clear my head."

Haley nodded, close to tears for the second time that evening. Same sadness, different brother.

Haley bent her head, touching her forehead to his. They stayed like that for a long time, until she finally said, "I'll see you tomorrow and we'll talk, okay?"

Scott pushed away from her and nodded, before walking away into the cold night.

***

In part because of what had happened with David and Scott, and also thanks to one game too many of beer pong, Haley spent the night tossing and turning in bed. Nightmares of zombies and vampires who alternately assumed the faces of either Scott or David tormented her all night, until she woke up in a pool of sweat.

She showered and ran to Scott's apartment with her hair still wet, not caring if David was there or not. When Scott opened the door, she threw herself into his arms and kissed him with a desperate passion. Without a word, he scooped her up into his arms and brought her to his bedroom, where they made love with that same desperation. And the physical closeness seemed to cure the argument.

Scott didn't bring up David anymore, and

Haley carefully avoided the topic as well. And if conversation felt stiff and tentative at first, they returned to normal interactions in a couple of days.

So, on the first Thursday of November, five days after the dreadful Halloween party, Haley headed toward Lavietes Pavilion with her roommates to watch the opening basketball game of the season: Harvard versus MIT. A super competitive game between next door neighbor schools. Jack had provided the tickets, and once inside the gym, Alice led them to their seats in the center bleacher only a few rows back from the basketball court.

"I need the restroom," Alice said as soon as she was out of her coat. "You guys need something from the concession stand?"

"No, I'm good, thanks," Madison said.

"Me, too," echoed Haley.

Alice left, and Haley concentrated on the players doing their warm-up drills... until her vision was blocked by a tall body.

"Hello, ladies." David had materialized in front of them, clad in a Crimson-supporter outfit: Harvard Crimson long-sleeved T-shirt and baseball hat, jeans, and sneakers. Popcorn in one hand, a soda in the other. "So nice of you to reserve me a spot."

Haley gasped. Her nostrils filled with his

familiar day-on-a-boat-out-at-sea scent, and she met his eyes for an instant before quickly looking away. Not that it saved her from receiving a Taser-like electric shock. David carried on as if nothing weird had happened between them, sliding in front of her to go sit next to Madison, one seat down from Haley.

"That's Alice's seat," Madison protested.

"Here." David lodged the soda between his legs and used his free hand to remove his baseball hat and throw it on the empty chair to his left. He wiggled on the seat to push aside Alice's coat as well. "She can take my spot. I like to sit in the middle."

"What are you doing here?" Madison insisted.

"Hey, I might not be on the team anymore, doesn't mean I'm not a fan."

Haley made a point of keeping her eyes trained on the court below them and not looking at him. It was too soon. For the past few days, she had purposely forbidden her brain from wandering anywhere near the David topic, but the fact remained that Scott had forced her to admit there was something between them. And now Haley's stupid heart wouldn't let her take it back.

"Oh, hello," Alice said, surprised when she came back to find her seat taken. "You're in my seat."

Haley made an effort to follow the

conversation, pretending she was looking—and thinking—elsewhere while she used her peripheral vision to track David's every movement.

He patted the chair next to him. "You've been moved to the left."

"Why don't *you* move to the left?"

"Come on, Alice, be nice. I promise I won't bite." Then he flashed her one of his most dashing smiles. "Popcorn?"

To Haley's dismay, Alice capitulated. She took a handful of popcorn and sat down just as the referee whistled to signal the game had started. They all followed the match in silence until about ten minutes in, when everyone around them, David included, shot up from the bleachers, yelling angrily against the referee.

Haley, Madison, and Alice were pretty much the only three people still seated in the whole stadium.

"What's going on?" Alice asked, once David was back in his seat.

"As the current and former girlfriend of two team captains, you know an awful little about the game."

"I hate watching sports. I'm a hero just for being here."

"Well, you came to see all Peter's games, so now you can't miss one of Jack's, can you?"

Alice glared at him.

"Oops, wasn't I supposed to say that? Are we pretending you and Peter never happened?"

"Why don't you harass someone else?"

"Well, your friend over there is doing all she can to pretend I don't exist." Haley did her best not to respond to the provocation, or even give notice she'd heard him. "And, as for Blondie here," David continued. "I've harassed her enough for a lifetime—"

"A-men," Madison interjected.

"So that leaves just the two of us," David concluded.

"I'm such a lucky girl." Alice scoffed. "On second thought, since I'm stuck with you…" Alice smacked David on the leg, just above the knee. "I always say the wrong thing to Jack after a game, and I have a feeling that if I say 'congratulations for winning' tonight, he'll bite my head off. Care to explain why, even though we're winning, Jack has his 'game-over' face on and Coach Morrison looks like he's about to have an apoplectic fit? If he shouts any louder, he'll spit out his vocal cords all the way over here."

Haley kept her eyes trained on the game, but that didn't stop her from eavesdropping on David and Alice. The truth was none of the girls understood much about basketball, and she, too, never knew how to talk to Scott after a game. So it'd be nice to have someone finally explain it all. Even if she couldn't openly acknowledge she was interested in what David was saying.

"Jack and the coach are mad because we're playing like crap," he explained.

"But we're ahead by twelve points. How can we be playing like crap and still lead by so much?"

"Well, that's easy: the other team is playing worse than us. If we were up against a half-decent team, they'd be hammering us."

"What are they doing wrong?"

"For starters, the new guy, number 1." David pointed at the court. "He has some big shoes to fill."

"Whose shoes?"

"Peter. He's replaced him as shooting guard—"

"Which is?"

"As the name suggests, the player who takes the most shots. He's usually the scoring leader, the MVP." David pointed to three imaginary spots as he spelled out each letter. "Most. Valuable. Player."

"And the guy isn't good?"

"Oh, no, the guy *is* good. But Peter was *phenomenal*. Let's just say this guy is not getting drafted by the NBA next year."

"I think I'm not gonna use that as a talking point with Jack."

David chuckled. "Wise girl."

"So what role is Jack playing?"

"Point guard. He's the game-maker, the one responsible for bringing the ball down the court and launching offensive plays. He directs the team."

"And he's doing a poor job?"

"No, the captain's the only one keeping up last year's standards."

Haley couldn't pretend not to be listening anymore. She turned toward David and asked, "Are you saying Scott's a bad player?"

"Hey, hello there." He waved at her.

Haley glared at him.

"I'm afraid Scotty isn't at his best tonight."

"What's his role?" Madison asked.

"Center. He's the team's muscle."

"So what's he doing wrong?" Haley asked.

"Almost everything tonight."

"Why?"

David studied the action taking place at the moment, his eyes roaming the court as they followed his brother around. Haley imitated him. MIT had the ball, and their number 12 was trying to find an opening into the Crimson defenses, that much was clear. The MIT guy with the ball passed it to a teammate close to Matt. This other guy caught the ball, feinted to the right, then sprung left instead, dribbled away from Matt, shot the ball toward the rim, and… missed. Scott jumped up in synchrony with another player from MIT, both of them reaching out for the ball… and the other guy got it, turned, and dunked it right into the hoop with both hands.

Admittedly, not Scott's best play. She turned to David to see if he had more of an insight.

David frowned, still studying the game. Finally, he whispered, "He's afraid."

"Afraid? Of what?"

"Of taking a hit to the head." David turned toward her. "He's supposed to be physically dominating the adversaries, getting the rebounds, blocking defenders, and opening other players up for driving to the basket… But look." He pointed to the court. "As soon as he sees as much as an elbow coming his way, he shies away."

"Oh." Haley was worried now. "It's the fall, isn't it?"

"Must be." David shrugged. "He never had this problem before."

"So what now?"

"If he keeps playing like that, the coach will bench him."

"Can you help him?"

David tilted his head to the side and studied her for a second or two with that impossibly sexy smirk of his. "When you ask it like that," he said, winking, "you know I can't say no."

Twelve

David

"Rise and shine," David announced in a sing-song voice, entering his brother's room on Sunday morning, three days after Scott's dreadful performance at Thursday's home game.

Scott was sleeping like a baby and barely stirred under the covers.

That won't do, David thought. With a vicious sense of satisfaction, he slid the blinds open and let the bright daylight do the dirty work for him.

True to expectations, Scott woke up with a groan, shouting, "Go away!" and trying to shield his eyes by burrowing his head under the sheets.

"Nah, ah, ah." David reached for the other end of the comforter and pulled in the opposite direction.

Scott jumped up into a sitting position and glared at him. The look could've worked, save that it was clear Scott still had morning foggy vision and couldn't properly focus on objects or people.

In fact, his brother rubbed his eyes before saying, "What's wrong with you?"

"C'mon, Scotty, you don't want to spend the

day in bed. The sun is shining and I'm dying to shoot a few hoops."

"What? You want to play basketball? No way."

"I've made you breakfast."

"Huh?"

"Breakfast is ready, the court is booked, and now all you have to do is get your ass out of bed." David snapped his fingers twice. "Chop, chop."

"David, I hate to break it to you, but the last thing I want to do today is play basketball. Practice and the games are enough, and Sunday is my day off."

David stared at the ceiling with the air of a martyr. "Well, I tried the sugar coated version…" He sat at the foot of the bed and patted his brother's legs. "If the simple joy of shooting a few hoops with your big brother isn't enough of an incentive, let me tell you how today is going to play out. You'll quit the Sleeping Beauty act, get out of bed, and eat the breakfast I prepared for you with all my brotherly love. Then you're coming with me to the gym, and we're going to play."

"Or else?"

David flared his nostrils. "Or else Coach Morrison is going to realize you're playing like a scared little girl and bench you for the rest of the season. Thursday night you were lucky MIT was full of crap. But the first team with a smidgen of talent is going to crush you, and you'll let them because you're afraid of a little confrontation. So today I'll rough you up until you're all set and good to go. Sound right?"

Scott shot him a glare. "It was *one* bad game."

"You missed nine rebounds out of ten. You got away with it once, but next time… Coach Morrison is going to catch on sooner or later. It took me about five minutes."

Scott finally threw the covers away and swung his feet off the bed. "What's this lovely breakfast you made?"

"Milk and cereal." David smirked, standing up.

"You've got to be kidding me," Scott said under his breath, getting out of bed.

"Hey, there's coffee, too."

***

The more awake Scott became, the more hostile he turned toward David. It was as if he'd remembered he was supposed to be mad at David but had forgotten in the few minutes after waking up. They ate breakfast in silence and walked to the gym in silence, the only sound that of the basketball David was bouncing off the concrete.

Once at their destination, David ran into the indoor court, putting on a little dribbling exhibition. Then he bounced the ball in a wide arc off the floor, leaped high, and slammed the thing. He caught the ball as it swished through the net and dribbled it back to where Scott was looking at him, unimpressed, from the midcourt line.

David and Scott stood in the center circle, facing each other like gladiators in the arena.

"You ready?" David asked.

"Do I have a choice?" Scott said.

"It's your life," David said, dropping the ball at Scott's feet.

"Yeah, it is." His brother picked up the ball while David spread his feet and arms, ready to defend.

David jerked his chin at the ball. "Let's see it."

Scott pulled up and let go of a twenty-footer.

Swish. It was in.

David ran to the basket to grab the ball and slung it back to Scott, then dropped back into his defensive stance. "C'mon, Scotty, that's cheating. We need to go *head* to *head*. Know what I mean?" David snickered.

Scott just blinked at him. Then he pulled up and sank another.

David retrieved the ball again. "That's how you wanna play it?" He resumed his position. "I've got all day."

Scott pulled up again and buried another one.

That was it. David gave him the ball again, but

this time he crowded right up next to Scott.

"What happened to all day?" Scott asked. Then he started to dribble, putting the ball on the floor for the first time since their mock game had started.

With a spurt forward, he drove for the basket, only to have David smack the ball away.

"Is that all you got, brother?" David taunted. "Because if that's your best game, you're benched for the rest of the season." With that, he slashed through the lane, shot, and scored.

Scott flared his nostrils, annoyed.

David fired the ball back at him. "Show me what you have."

Scott dribbled, feinted right and darted left, but David saw the move coming and was on him in an instant, taking the ball away again. He pivoted on his heels, bolted for the basket, and scored again. And again. And again. And again.

"Is your butt already getting comfortable on the bench?" David taunted, before he flung the ball back at his brother.

As soon as his fingers had a secure grip on the ball, an enraged Scott charged at him like a bull. He threw a shoulder into his chest and spun hard, catching David's nose with a vicious elbow thrust. David bent at the waist, holding his nose with his hand as a few droplets of blood dripped down. In the background, he heard the ball swish past the net.

"You had enough?"

Scott's angry voice made him turn.

"Why stop now?" David asked, pulling up the bottom of his tank top to wipe his face. "You're just starting to get the gist of it."

Scott pushed the ball on his chest. "Be my guest, but you won't score again."

David snickered. Then he backed off and worked a crossover dribble, trying to set his brother up. He faked left. And when Scott leaned, David darted right. He went past Scott in a flash, gaining a straight shot to the basket. David leaped and let go of a sweet finger roll. But before it reached its height, Scott pinned it against the backboard, blocking David's action. And the next. And the next. And the next.

David came down from another failed jump and stared at his brother. "Look who's back."

Scott glared at him.

"Is that all the gratitude I get for helping you?"

"Helping me?" Scott discarded the ball to the side with an angry throw and marched on him. "Were you also trying to help me on Halloween?" He shoved David back with both hands.

David staggered a few steps backward. "Uh-oh. Someone is pouty…"

"Stay the hell away from me, David, and from her." Scott glowered at him one last time, adding,

"I mean it." Then he stormed out of the gym.

"You're welcome," David whispered to the thin air.

Haley

"I'm about to make a proposal that might be very unpopular," Alice announced, coming into the living room.

It was Friday afternoon and, instead of gearing up for an evening out, the girls were all wearing sweatpants, ready to watch the Stanford vs Harvard game on TV that was scheduled to start in less than an hour at 5 p.m. Crazy as it sounded, the game was neither in California or Massachusetts, but it would take place in Shanghai. Apparently, both the Crimson and the Cardinal wanted to do a little brand-building, despite being already well-known internationally.

"What is it?" Haley asked, just as Madison said, "If you're about to suggest we renounce popcorn because it's not healthy, you're out."

"It's not food related," Alice said.

Both Haley and Madison stared up at her expectantly.

"I thought," Alice said, wringing her hands, "we could invite David over to watch the game with us."

The proposition earned Haley's roommate two sets of raised brows.

"Before you say 'no,' hear me out." Alice raised her palms to forestall any protest. "I know you both have your issues with him, but… He was really useful last week when he explained everything that was going on play-by-play. First time I could talk to Jack about a game. And David's probably going to watch the game anyway… so I figured…"

"I don't think it's a good idea," Haley said unequivocally.

She hadn't told the girls about Halloween. If she had, she was sure Alice would've never proposed anything like that. And she wasn't planning on telling them now, but still, David in her house, while Scott was away, was a big, fat *no!*

Unfortunately, Madison had the opposite reaction. She shrugged and said, "I don't mind. If we have to watch the damn game, we might as well understand what's going on. It's so boring when we can only count the points."

With one roommate convinced, Alice turned to Haley with a pleading expression. "Please? David really helped last time…" Haley was about to say 'no' again when Alice continued with her argument. "What if he's watching the game at home all alone and sad?"

Haley scowled. "Think more at a bar and with a girl on his arm."

Alice switched to a passive-aggressive approach. "Okay, if you don't want to, I'll drop it."

Haley puffed her cheeks up and let the air out in an impatient huff. "How important is this to you?"

Alice joined her hands in prayer. "Very, very important. Crucial to my relationship's health."

"Oh, come on," Madison said, coming to Alice's aid. "The game is more fun when David's explaining it."

True.

But you have unexplored feelings for the guy, a voice retorted inside Haley's head. *Best to avoid him.*

Also true.

But if she said 'no' now, the girls would sense she wasn't telling them something. And Haley really didn't want to have to explain the whole Halloween drama now. Better to say 'yes' and hope David would refuse. It was Friday night, after all, he probably already had plans. Yes, he'd definitely say 'no.'

Wrong!

Less than half an hour later their doorbell rang, and David waltzed into the house carrying a Coors

Light six-pack and four pizza boxes.

"Hello, ladies, I come bearing gifts." He dropped everything on the coffee table. "I have beers and I have pizza. Double cheese, pepperoni, and two regulars. You get your pick."

"Amen," Madison said, launching herself at one of the pizza boxes.

Haley stole a glance at him and cursed herself for the tiny electric jolt meeting his blue eyes gave her. In response, David's mouth curled up at one corner as if he'd just read her mind. He winked at her before sitting comfortably on the couch between her and Alice.

Haley tried to make herself small and shrink away as much as she could. But nothing could shield her from his conspicuous presence next to her… Hell, this was going to be a long evening.

***

"Can you believe the team had to go to China to play a game?" Madison asked during the half-time break. "I mean, freaking China! It's a different continent."

"At least they'll be home for Christmas this year," Alice said. "I couldn't have afforded another trip to Hawaii."

"So what are you doing?" Madison asked. "Aren't your parents going on their usual

Christmas cruise?"

Alice beamed at them. "Going home with Jack. He's already invited me. I guess I'm meeting the parents."

"Ugh, I'm getting diabetes just looking at you," Madison said jokingly, then turned to Haley. "And what about you?"

"Yeah," David said, inserting himself into the conversation. "Are you coming home to *meet the parents?*"

He stared at her with a half-challenging, half-mocking little smirk. The fact that going home with Scott to meet his parents would mean also spending the holidays with David, in the same house, was not lost on Haley.

She'd already met their mother in a brief encounter back in August while Scott was still hospitalized. But to spend the holidays at the Williams' house would be a whole different ball game.

"I haven't discussed it with Scott yet," Haley said, choosing a neutral reply. "But I can't bail on my parents for two Christmases in a row, especially not after this summer."

"Oh, right," Madison said.

David only mouthed a cocksure "Pity" at her.

"The game's back on," Alice said, grabbing the remote and turning up the volume. "Come on, guys, we're only two points down."

The words had barely left her lips when Stanford scored again.

"Only four points down?" Alice said, dismayed. "Why are we doing such a poor job?"

"We're letting them take the lead," David said. "It's always them going ahead, and us trying to catch up. Our defense sucks."

"Is it Scott's fault?" Haley asked.

"In part," David confirmed.

"Is he still afraid?"

"No, I cured that. But he's angry, and he's making poor judgment calls."

"Angry about what?"

David turned to look at her. "I don't know, you tell me. Trouble in paradise?"

"No!" Haley wasn't about to discuss her relationship issues with the guy who was causing them.

"Then Scott must be wearing his angry *mask* for no reason," David replied, putting extra strain on the word 'mask' to let her know he wasn't buying any of her bullshit.

Haley shot him a not-taking-the-bait look and concentrated on the game, which, from then on, only got worse. So far, Harvard had managed to keep in pursuit of the Cardinal within a margin of four to five points, but the gap started increasing to eight, ten, and even twelve points toward the end.

With only ten seconds left on the clock, Harvard was down by nine. Not ready to give up, Jack was slashing through the lane in a last attempt to bring home two more points, but the referee blew his whistle three times before he could shoot. The game was over.

"And that, ladies," David said in a resigned tone, "is how you lose."

Thirteen

Haley

Scott didn't come back from China until late next Sunday night. With midterms so close, they could only hang out together to study. So, on Monday, they met at a private study room at the library. Scott barely kissed her hello before opening a biology textbook and burying his nose in it. Since they had to do homework, it made sense not to talk much, but Haley sensed Scott's silence went beyond that. It felt… hostile.

Initially, Haley pinned the bad mood on the lost game against Stanford. After all, who'd be happy to fly fifteen hours to China only to lose in front of thousands of local spectators and even more college basketball aficionados back home? But, according to David, Scott had been playing like crap because he'd been angry… So if he'd started the match already in a bad temper, losing would only have aggravated the issue, but it wasn't the cause…

Haley shifted in her chair. "Are you sure you're okay?" she asked, for what must've been the third time.

"Yes."

"Is it basketball?"

"No."

"So you're not having any trouble playing?"

Scott kept his eyes trained on the pre-med textbook he was highlighting. "What's that supposed to mean?"

"Seems you have a harder time defending since… the accident…"

"And since when have you become a basketball expert?"

"I'm not, but David said—"

Scott's neck snapped up so fast Haley thought it might break. "David? When did you see him?"

"We watched the games together."

"Games, plural?"

"He came to the MIT game. It's a public space," Haley added defensively, seeing his dark look. "And Alice invited him to our place to watch the Stanford game. She needed someone to explain what was going on with the game so she could discuss it with Jack later, and David is the only person we know who understands basketball."

"Why didn't you tell me?" Scott demanded.

"Wow, Scott, calm down, do I have to fill in a log every time I see David now?"

"You shouldn't be seeing him at all."

"What? Are you going to have to approve all of my friends now?"

"David is not your friend, as you made very clear on Halloween."

There. The resentment that had kept bubbling under the surface since Halloween was finally seeping through the cracks. No matter if they hadn't discussed it, or pretended the issue didn't exist. David's shadow was always with them. And it made Haley feel so angry and so guilty.

"So David is on the list of people I can't see. What's next? Are you going to pick the clothes I can wear?"

Scott stared at her, shocked. "That's not fair, Haley, I'm not some jealous psycho. What would you do in my place? Would it be okay for you if I hung out with a girl who..." Scott trailed off, apparently unable to frame what the equivalent would be. A girl he liked? A girl he had feelings for? What had he wanted to say?

"Listen. For the MIT game, David just showed up at the gym and sat between Alice and Madison. I could either go and miss the game, or stay and not make a big deal out of it. And for the Stanford game, Alice invited him to our place, and—"

"You could've said 'no!'"

"I did, but she insisted so much it would've been weird if I kept saying 'no.' I would've had to explain..." This time Haley left the phrase hanging.

"Explanations are hard, aren't they?" Scott

said, his tone bitter.

He looked down at his hands and kept silent for the longest time. When he finally lifted his gaze, his eyes were all red and shiny. "I can't do this, Haley. Not anymore…"

Haley's body reacted as if she were free-falling, even while sitting perfectly still in her chair. She stared at Scott filled with dread and, oddly enough, relief. Since Halloween, something had shifted in their relationship, even if they'd both pretended everything was the same. David had been on her mind more often than not, and Scott seemed to have picked up on her indecision, even if he hadn't said a word about it. Until now.

"Come on, Haley," Scott continued. "We're past you trying to spare my feelings… You can admit it."

"Over the summer…" Haley paused to gather her thoughts. "Something changed… between David and me."

"When you found out about the kiss?"

"Maybe that was the start, but then it became much more than it ever used to be. I never had real feelings for him, not even after the kiss. And I never lied to you, and I don't want to lie now…"

"So what happened?" Scott's voice shook. "What changed?"

Haley looked at him with teary eyes. "You went away," she admitted. "In the beginning, I missed you so much… But all summer we spent days without having a meaningful conversation… Whenever I called, you were too busy to talk, or it wasn't the right moment. That is, if you even picked up the phone at all. It never seemed like you missed me… and I guess because of it, I sort of stopped missing you… It felt like you weren't there for me, not just physically, but emotionally, too…"

"And David was?"

Haley swallowed and nodded. "With you gone, it was like I couldn't breathe anymore… But David… he bulldozed his way into my life and forced me to let the air in again… and my first gasp of it was a big laugh."

"So it was all my fault… because I left?" Scott said, again not angry, only bitter. "You're saying I practically drove you to him… He told me, you know?"

"Told you what?"

"That he was gonna steal you while I was gone. I just never thought you would've let David into your heart…" Scott paused, then asked, "What is it exactly that you like about him? I mean, I get it, he was there when your dad got sick, but…" Scott stared at her, at a loss for words.

"David makes everything feel new and… unpredictable. I'm a different person with him. He changes me, challenges me, and… surprises me.

When we're together, I'm no longer sure of anything. He makes me question everything. When I'm with him… it's like… I'm free."

"And I'm your cage?"

"Not a cage. With you, I feel loved and safe and protected."

"And are those such bad things?"

"No, just different things."

"Things you don't want anymore…"

"Scott… I'm sorry. I never wished for any of this. It just happened. I hadn't even fully realized it until—"

"Yeah, exactly when did you realize you had feelings for my brother?"

A million flashbacks passed through Haley's mind, followed by just as many questions. *The day he told me about the kiss? All those afternoons together at the library? When he drove me home to my father? The night he gave me this necklace?* Haley's hand unconsciously wrapped around it. *When he saved you from the pool? When he stayed up all night to read to you at the hospital? When I found out he wouldn't let Madison tell me about his apology to her? On Halloween night?*

All of those moments had made her fall for him a little, but the truth of it was all in a single instant spent together under the rain. *"I won't go away, Haley."* David's words rang again in her mind. *"I'll always be here for you… I love you."*

"Last summer," Haley confessed. "He told me he loved me—"

Scott scoffed. "I guess that's another little thing you conveniently forgot to tell me."

"No, I chose not to."

"Why?"

"I didn't want to come between two brothers…"

"Yeah, great job with that."

"I'm sorry."

"Why drag it out for so long if you've known for months?" he accused.

"Because I didn't *know*-know. Because it was all so confusing. And because I still love you. Before I could start thinking about the way I felt for David, you came back, and I was so happy to see you… Then there was the accident, and that day at the hospital I was so scared to lose you… I thought whatever I'd imagined having with David had to be… nothing real, nothing important…"

"And now?"

"Now I don't know what I want anymore…"

"What, or… who you want?"

Haley kept silent.

"Did you two ever…?"

"No, Scott, no! How can you ask me that? I would never cheat on you."

"At this point I don't really know, do I?"

"I'm sorry."

"For what? Because you want him?"

"It's more complicated than that. There isn't a switch I can turn that says 'stop loving Scott, love David instead.'"

"Love? You *love* him?"

Haley could only stare back at Scott.

"And you love me, too?"

She nodded.

"But you're in love with only one of us…"

Fourteen

Madison

A quick peek at her watch told Madison that Scott was already twenty minutes late, which was pretty unusual for him. They'd reserved a study room at the library to finish the next revision of their group project and, with the assignment due tomorrow, they really couldn't afford to waste any time.

The project—a co-written short story that had to be cohesive, but with two clear, distinct voices—had been presented in their second class, and Madison and Scott had teamed up at once. Now they were halfway through, with Madison writing in the POV of a young witch, while Scott penned her very sarcastic talking cat.

Fed up with just sitting there and waiting, Madison started revising her side of the story. And by the time Scott arrived, she was so immersed in the narrative that he startled her when he plunged into the chair next to her.

"Sorry I'm late."

Late, Madison scoffed inside her head. *What a pity we're not working on euphemisms.*

She was about to berate Scott for letting her do all the work when she took a second look at him:

one-day stubble, dark sunglasses, messed up hair, and a foul reek of…

"Are you *drunk?*" she accused.

Scott sneered. "Mostly hungover."

Madison's eyes bulged. "But it's the middle of the day. Are you okay?"

"Haley and I broke up. By definition, I'm not *okay.*"

A million different thoughts and emotions hit Madison in the guts like sudden punches: elation, guilt, sorrow, hope, elation again, followed by the same guilt. Then, finally, the need to know exactly what had happened. Who had broken up with who, and why?

"How can it be?" she asked

"So you haven't talked to her?"

"No. Last night she came home and shut herself in her room. We assumed she had homework to do or something… What happened?"

"Apparently…" Scott removed the sunglasses and, elbows on the table, he pressed both his palms against his closed eyes. "She has feelings for my brother."

Ah, yeah, there's that…

Scott finished rubbing his eyes and turned his bloodshot gaze to her, studying her reaction. "And you don't seem surprised."

"Scott, I—"

"Please," Scott interrupted her. "If you're about to spin me some bullshit, don't. I've already had enough of that."

"I wasn't going to, but Haley is my best friend…"

"And what about me? Am I not your friend?"

Oh, Scott, you're so much more than that.

"Of course we're friends, but—"

"No buts. Did you know she had feelings for David, or not?"

"I suspected it, but the one time I confronted her about it, she denied it."

"Why did you confront her?"

"Because I'd seen them together."

"Where?"

"At the library."

"Damn, I hate libraries." Scott stared around the room with contempt. "What were they doing?"

Madison cursed herself for not being able to keep a poker face. The interrogation was making her so uncomfortable. She didn't want to spill the beans on Haley, but… Scott deserved to know the truth.

"Nothing, really," she explained. "They weren't doing anything specific except for laughing." Scott's face turned even grimmer, as if instead of "laughing" Madison had just said they were banging each other's brains out on the table. "It was more of a vibe I picked up."

"And when you confronted her about it, what did she say?"

She pivoted the argument on me for having feelings for you... Yeah, definitely not going to say that.

"She swore they were only friends," Madison said as neutrally as she could.

"Yeah. Just fucking friends."

"Scott." Madison put a hand on his arm. "I don't think she was lying. Not consciously, at least."

"When did I lose her? When she learned about the kiss?"

"No, that night she was only worried about how you'd react when she told you. She still hated David back then…"

"So when did it change?"

"I guess when they started meeting at the library. David… he can be charming if he wants to…"

"Okay, now I seriously despise libraries. Can we get outta here?"

Madison threw a glance at their half-finished story… Homework didn't matter right then.

"Yeah," she said, pressing Save before closing her laptop. "Let's go."

Scott stared at the computer, aghast. "Oh, I'm so sorry, the project! I wasn't thinking straight. We can stay and finish it."

"No, it doesn't matter, really." Madison shrugged. "We were almost done, anyway."

"I don't want you to have to finish alone."

"Scott, you're having enough of a bad day to also worry about homework. Trust me. Let's get out of here."

Scott held her gaze for a long moment. "Thank you."

Outside, they walked in silence in the freezing November air with no particular destination. Wrapped in a heavy coat and shielded by a wooly beanie, scarf, and mittens, Madison still couldn't help shivering a little. But Scott seemed immune to the cold. He wore no hat, scarf, or gloves, and kept his jacket with the first two or three buttons undone, but he didn't seem to feel the bite of the wind.

Scott spoke first. "Do you think it would've been different if I hadn't gone to California?" He stared into space straight ahead, as if searching the horizon for an answer.

"Hard to call…"

Scott stopped walking and turned toward her. "You went out with David. What did you like about him?"

Madison reflexively widened her eyes at the blunt question. "You really want me to answer that?"

"Probably not, you're right. But when you two

broke up you hated him, too, right? And now you don't anymore… How does he do that? How can he be such a douchebag to everyone, and people just keep on giving him chances…"

Madison stared up at him in surprise, a fierce blush heating up her cheeks. Did Scott know about her breakup with David?

"Nobody told me anything," Scott clarified. "But I can pick up on things… at least when other people are involved. Guess I'm not as good at reading my own girlfriend—sorry, *ex*-girlfriend."

Madison started walking again. "I did hate him for a time…"

Scott fell into step next to her. "And then?"

"He apologized."

"You think he was sincere?"

"I do."

"You never suspected it was just a move?"

"To look good for Haley? Oh, yeah, I did. And I told him, so he asked me not to tell Haley about the apology to let me know it was all about me…"

"And did you?"

"What?"

"Tell Haley."

"Not at first…"

"But eventually?"

"Yeah."

"When?"

Madison was reluctant to answer.

"When?" Scott repeated.

"The day after the accident… David was reading to you at the hospital, and I made a joke about him torturing you with bad fiction, so Haley asked me if I still hated him, and I said 'no' and told her why."

"So I go into a coma and he gets extra hero points for saving my life, and also for apologizing to you… no matter he had to apologize because he was a total shitbag in the first place. Why does everyone prefer him?"

It was Madison's turn to stop. "I don't prefer him. Scott, I can barely tolerate your brother. I'm… I can't even say. Haley must be out of her mind to choose him over you."

Scott stared at her, slightly open-mouthed, and if Madison's cheeks were heated before, they were about to melt right now.

Why don't I come out and tell him I'm in love with him? I mean, I only have to spell it out for him for it to be any clearer.

"You really think that?" he asked.

"Yeah, he's… *David,* and you're you, and there really is an ocean between the two."

"You say that only because we share the same weird literary tastes."

"Absolutely. You're the only guy I know crazy enough to write about a talking cat."

Out of the blue, Scott pulled her into a hug.

"Thank you, Madison," he whispered. "I was a drunken mess before talking to you, but you made it better."

Madison let herself get lost in the embrace, feeling a bit stalkerish. Scott was hugging her as a friend, and instead, she was savoring the warmth of his body pressed close to hers while her heart raced out of control in her chest. His strong arms wrapped around her… his lips almost kissing her hair…

That's it! You've been enough of a perv for tonight.

"Hey," Madison said, using all her will to pull back. "It's what friends are for."

***

That evening, after saying goodbye to Scott and going back to the library to finish their project—it took every ounce of Madison's willpower to plow through the revisions, considering all her brain wanted to think about was: Scott is single, Scott is single, Scott is single—Madison finally made it home way later than she'd planned.

"Oh, there you are," Alice greeted her. She was making grilled cheese sandwiches in the kitchenette. "Where were you?"

"Is Haley home?" Madison whispered, ignoring the question.

"Yeah, why?" Alice whispered back.

Madison stalled by removing her coat and various anti-freeze props and hanging them on the entrance hall's rack. Before she told Alice, she wanted to make sure she wasn't going to smile. Madison hated herself for being so happy about the breakup, but she couldn't help herself. Yeah, Scott was miserable, and seeing him so beaten down had been heartbreaking, but he would recover and maybe… just maybe… And Haley… it wasn't like her best friend was going to be alone for long… she was probably already dating David…

Madison schooled her face in a grievous expression and joined Alice in the kitchen.

"So, apparently Haley and Scott broke up."

"WHAT?!"

"Shhhhhh," Madison hissed. "She'll hear you."

"What?" Alice hissed.

"Scott and I were supposed to work on our group project today, but he turned up an hour late looking like a mess… he was half drunk and one hundred percent out of it."

"And why did they break up?" Alice asked, copying Madison's hush-hush tones.

"She has feelings for David."

"Ah," was all Alice said. No surprises there.

"Have you seen her?"

"No."

Madison chewed on her lower lip. "Should we check on her?"

As one, they nodded and moved in front of Haley's door.

Alice knocked, saying, "Can we come in?"

No reply came from the other side, so they shared another let's-do-this glance and then tentatively opened the door. Haley was lying on the bed, fully clothed, legs crossed at the ankles, gaze lost on the ceiling. She had earplugs on and it took her a moment to realize she was no longer alone.

"Hey." Haley removed the earplugs and straightened up, crossing her legs. She took one look at their serious expressions, and said, "So you've heard."

They joined her on the bed, sitting on opposite sides.

"How are you?" Alice asked.

Haley blinked. "Dazzled, to be honest... I didn't cry."

Madison frowned. "And that is bad because...?"

"I'm numb. It's like I can't feel anything... and I'm scared it's only a matter of time before I realize what a horrible mistake I made and my heart is going to get ripped out of my chest."

Madison didn't have a response to that. She

could only agree, for obvious reasons. But Alice seemed at a loss for words as well.

"How did you find out?" Haley finally asked.

To which Madison blushed for the millionth time that day.

"You saw him," Haley guessed. "How was he?"

"A mess," Madison said. "But he was… functioning." It was the only word Madison could think of to describe the state Scott had been in.

"Does he hate me?"

Madison shook her head. "No, he's still very much in love with you…"

Haley's mouth twisted into a grief-stricken, possibly guilt-tripping grimace.

"I'm sorry," she said.

"Hey." Alice reached out to grab her hand. "It's a breakup, not the end of the world. But are you sure it's what you want?"

Alice had asked the question Madison dared not voice, too afraid of the answer.

"I mean," Alice continued, "this was rather sudden. You never said a word. What happened?"

Haley told them the behind-the-scenes of "Haley and The Williams Brothers" that had taken place on Halloween night. And how she and Scott had both pretended none of it had happened for two weeks. But how, yesterday, at the mere mention of David's name, he'd flipped and Haley hadn't been able to deny she had feelings for both brothers.

"It wasn't fair to keep going," she concluded. "Scott deserves a person who's one hundred percent into him, and I couldn't be that person anymore."

"So… have you seen David yet?" Madison asked.

"No, and I'm not sure I'm ready yet. I need space… Alice?"

"Yeah?"

"Can you make sure Jack keeps an eye on Scott? With basketball going to shit and us breaking up, I'm worried he'll flip out…"

"Sure, no problem," Alice said. Then, seeing how Haley still seemed completely zoned out, she added, "Hey, it's going to be fine. Scott's going to be fine."

"I know, but the last thing I wanted was to come between two brothers, especially after their history with girls. It's true that relationships come and go, but family should be forever. They're brothers, and no matter how they act, deep down they love each other and would go to the end of the world for each other. I mean, did you see how crazy David went that day at the pool?"

"Yep," Madison and Alice said in unison.

"I don't want to ruin their bond, but I'm afraid I did exactly that."

The three of them stared at each other, neither sure how much truth Haley's words held.

Fifteen

David

After a long day of school, David came home glad he'd toughened up with an investment banking internship over summer break. All his fellow HBS students seemed so stressed about their projects, midterms, and deadlines, but for David, business school felt more like a vacation after the summer he'd had and his nightmare of an ex-boss.

He turned the key in the lock and pushed the entrance door open. Or, at least, he tried. Something heavy was blocking the way on the other side. David did some extra shoving and, finally, he was able to open the door enough to sneak into his own house through the crack. He closed the door behind him and inspected the tower of boxes that had been blocking it. There were five carton boxes in total with various names written in blue marker: tech, kitchen, bath, bed, and mix.

A quick look around the apartment notified David of all the new empty spaces: no coffee machine in the kitchen, no stereo in the living room, the Michael Jordan poster gone… All of Scott's stuff. And, at last, David's gaze settled on the two big suitcases parked behind the couch just as Scott emerged from his room, rolling another bag in place to join the others.

"Going somewhere?" David asked.

Scott shot him an unreadable look. "Yeah."

"Where to this time? Alaska?"

"Nope," Scott said, standoffish. "Just a couple of blocks down the road."

With that, his brother walked back into his room, presumably to finish packing. David leaned against the kitchen bar column, crossed his arms over his chest, and waited. He watched as Scott reemerged from his bedroom with yet another box and filled it with the last few of his possessions still scattered around the house.

"Listen," David said. "I'm all for you claiming your independence and flying away from the nest, but how are you going to afford to live on your own?"

"I'm not going to."

"Okay, then. What about the rent here?"

Scott dropped the box and turned to face him. "I'm switching with Matt. He's moving in with you, and I'll go live with Jack. The rent is about the same, so I'll keep paying my half here and Matt will pay for his place, but we're swapping."

"Well," David said, taken aback. "Thank you for consulting me. I have nothing against the dude, but shouldn't you have at least asked if I was okay living with him?"

"No."

"No?"

"No."

"What's going on? Why the sudden change?" David raised an arm and sniffed underneath his armpit. "I don't stink, I promise."

"Obviously you haven't heard." Scott took a step forward. "Haley and I broke up."

"Oh."

The two brothers stared at each other for a long time, a non-verbal communication of mixed emotions passing between them. Scott visibly angry, bitter, and so freakily calm David worried he was going to go Charlie Manson on him. And David, trying to keep a straight face while his heart was pounding in his chest. He didn't like to see his brother this way, but…

"You want to blow off steam?" David suggested. "Go get drunk, brother-bond over a good old Irish ale?"

Scott eyed him in an I-dare-you sort of way. "Let's not pretend for a second like this isn't the best day of your life," he said, glacially cold. "I'm going out."

"Where?"

Scott pulled on his coat. "Out."

"All right, I won't wait up for you."

"Yeah, don't," Scott said, just before

slamming the door shut behind him.

David grabbed a beer from the fridge and, after knocking it open on the countertop, he crashed on the couch, taking a sip. So Haley was single… What did that mean?

He pulled his phone out of his jeans pocket and checked it for texts. Not a peep. Mmm. He toyed with the phone for a while. He didn't want to make a move on Haley while his brother's body was still warm, but he'd already waited for so long… But what to do? Write a text? Ask her out? Nah… too simple… he needed to come up with something special. But then, he'd never been one for grand gestures, and at this point, all that really mattered were Haley's feelings. Either she was into him, or she wasn't. Maybe, in this case, less was more… all he needed was an opportunity.

Haley

David.

Haley's breath caught in her throat as she walked out of her last class of the day and spotted him waiting on the other side of the road. He had the frozen-over air of someone who'd been waiting out in the cold for a long time: red nose, beanie pulled down almost to cover his eyes, and arms tightly wrapped around himself to keep warm.

She crossed over to him. "David."

"Still me."

"How long have you been here?"

"Scott told me about the breakup. I'd say I'm sorry, but I'm not."

Ah, so they weren't circling around it.

"What did he say?"

"Oh, you know my brother. He's a real talker..." David rolled his eyes. "The guy just went on and on about it. Wouldn't shut up."

"So he didn't tell you why?"

"Nope." David moved a step closer. "Why don't you tell me?"

"I'm not in love with him anymore." Haley chose the easier half of the truth. She couldn't tell David she loved him, not yet... It was all still too confusing.

"Mmm..." David's mouth curled up into a little, satisfied smile. "Interesting... Anyone else on your mind?"

Oh, gosh, if he kept looking at her like this Haley was sure she'd melt.

She swallowed. "Can we not do this right now?"

"Too soon?"

Haley nodded. "I need space, and we can't do this to him so soon..."

David's smile widened, and he closed the distance between them. "So, Miss Robot." He cupped her cheeks. "There's a 'we,' is there? And what was that you were thinking of *not* doing?"

Haley couldn't help but smile.

He held her gaze for a long time, his thumbs caressing her skin. He pressed closer, making Haley gasp.

"You want to kiss me," he said. It was a realization, not a question.

"Yes," Haley said.

"Good." David leaned in closer but pressed his lips only to her forehead. Then his mouth moved to whisper in her ear. "Pity I have to give you space."

Shivers that had nothing to do with the cold weather spider-walked down Haley's spine, and there was a warm explosion in her lower belly. Heart pounding, she stared up into his teasing blue eyes. Coherent speech abandoned her, and Haley felt very much ready to throw all precautions out the window and grab him by the collar of his coat to kiss him. But David stepped back.

"Don't get too comfortable," he said. "I'll come knocking on your door soon." And with that he walked away, leaving her all hot and bothered in the middle of the street.

***

He didn't call or text the next day, nor the next, nor the next. He didn't wait for her outside another class, either, until days of radio silence turned into weeks. Before Haley realized it, November was gone and finals week was looming over them.

Not even an impatient heart could keep a Harvard student from studying. Well, not exactly. Haley's revision was only half-disrupted by nagging thoughts of David, doubling the time it took to get anything done.

Why couldn't she push him out of her mind? He was ignoring her, and it bothered her. But he was only doing as she'd asked, leaving her space. So why was she so mad at him?

You should make the next move, an insistent voice whispered in her head.

True.

David had laid it all bare last summer. Haley knew where he stood. Now she had to tell him where her heart was… with him. Ah… but knowing what one should do and actually doing it were two completely different things. So, instead, Haley buried her head under the sand—or under coding textbooks, in this case—and concentrated on passing her finals with top grades.

With the examinations over, it was time to go home to Buffalo. And now it was too late to talk to David. She didn't want to have the "I love you, too" conversation and then have to leave and not see him for two weeks.

I'll clear my head over the break and call David when I come back, Haley promised herself.

Her last night in Cambridge was spent, as was tradition, with her roommates, swapping presents. They sat on the living room rug next to their plastic Christmas tree, each with two gift-wrapped bundles in front of them. Blue, Alice's bunny, was comfortably snuggled under the tree, sleeping.

"Should we take turns, or open them all at once?" Madison asked.

"All at once," Alice said.

"Yeah," Haley agreed.

"Okay, ready… go!" Madison yelled, and the unwrapping frenzy began.

Haley opened Madison's present first. There was a book: *The Night of Wishes* by Michael Ende. Whenever Madison gave a gift, no matter the occasion, it was always a novel—to spread the book love—plus something else. Haley peeked at the first page to read the dedication:

A Christmas story with a talking

cat… to keep your mind off boys.

Haley smiled and opened the second bit of the present. A brand-new phone case in a gorgeous shade of red. Haley's old one was all battered and scratched.

"Thank you, Maddie," Haley said. "I love it."

"And I love yours." Madison held up her "I read past my bedtime" throw pillow in front of her. It had a silver background made of an antique-looking calligraphy and the main writing was pink.

"What did Alice get you?" Haley asked.

"TA starter set," Madison said proudly, showing off her new stationery supply kit. "I still can't believe Professor McKenna offered me a position for next year." Madison paused and chewed on her lower lip. "Now all I have to do is tell my dad I'm not going to law school."

"It'll be fine," Alice reassured her, wielding a rose gold makeup brush in the air, whose handle was in the shape of a mermaid tail.

Once the various books, accessories, makeup tools, and house décor items were unpacked, Alice got up and asked, "Hot chocolate with marshmallows? Raise your hands if you're in."

Two hands promptly shot into the air.

Alice came back five minutes later with three steaming mugs in her hands. She handed them each one and then, teary-eyed, she said, "A toast." She raised her mug. "Living with you guys has been the best… I don't know where we'll be next year… if we'll keep living in the same apartment, or even in the same city. But I wanted to say you're my best friends… and that's never going to change… Cheers!"

All three definitely shiny-eyed, they bumped mugs, yelling, "Cheers!"

Haley sipped her hot cocoa and stared out of the window at the snowflakes lazily making their way to the ground, feeling overwhelmed by how much her life was about change… not just at the end of the year after graduation, but in a little over two weeks when she'd be back and ready to talk to David.

Sixteen

Scott

"MOM!" David shouted from the top of the stairs. "Why is there a gym in my bedroom?"

Scott and his brother had just gotten home early on Christmas Eve after a short—unfortunately, shared—car ride from Boston to Poughkeepsie. The four-hour door-to-door trip had been the most Scott had seen of David since he'd moved out of their apartment, and he'd already had enough. He'd considered taking the bus home, but then he would've had to explain to his parents why he couldn't stand to be in a car with his brother, and that would've been even more unbearable.

But at least it was going to be a short stay. The team had the last game of the year scheduled for the thirtieth, and Scott had claimed he had to be back in Boston on the twenty-seventh, meaning he would leave here the day after Christmas.

When they'd arrived home, David had said a quick hello to their parents and then hurried up to the second floor, taking the stairs two at a time, to drop his bag. But now he was standing on the landing, arms crossed over his chest, looking at their mother with a questioning frown.

"Oh, dear," their mom—a five-foot-two woman nobody believed could've produced two such tall boys—said. "I forgot to tell you we've redecorated. You guys are in the guest room."

"Together?" Scott asked.

"Yeah, you're going to bunk together, just like old times."

Perfect, Scott thought, while trying to keep a straight face. Being under the same roof with David again would already be difficult, but to share a room would be… *hell!*

He crept up the stairs carrying his duffle bag. First he checked his old room, hoping their mother had gotten confused and only David's room had been re-purposed. But, no, as soon as he opened the door, that hope was lost. In place of his twin bed was a huge mahogany desk, and his old desk and wardrobe had been replaced by neatly organized bookshelves. The whole room held a distinct feminine vibe: pale colors, assorted flower pots, and medicinal herbs posters hung on the walls instead of his Metallica ones. So if David's room had become a gym, his was now Mom's home office.

Sighing, Scott closed the door and headed for the guest room, taking in with grim resignation the matching set of twin beds on opposite sides of the room. The headboards seemed to have been laser cut in the middle and split in two, meaning the beds might be pushed together and become one, depending on the guests.

David had already claimed the bed by the window.

"I picked the window seat," David said, turning as Scott dropped his bag on the free bed. "You mind?"

"Whatever," he said, and then got out of there as fast as he could.

The house wasn't big, but large enough that he could limit unnecessary David-interactions to a minimum. Scott only hoped his parents wouldn't pick up on the lingering tension. More like parent, singular; his dad had never been able to read the nuances of his kids' behavior. But Mom… she was a different animal.

Dinner was painful to endure. They didn't see their parents that often, so there was little chance they'd let them go quickly. Small talk and David's presence had to be endured. Scott did his best to be polite and pretend he was doing great: in school, with the team… Luckily, no one asked about his non-existent girlfriend. Admittedly, he took a more passive approach to the conversation, answering questions directed at him and never initiating an exchange. But that was his all-out best.

Hours later, in the dark of their shared

bedroom, the oppressive silence made it clear neither of the two brothers was sleeping. When Scott couldn't take it any longer, he asked, "So... you've seen Haley around?"

David's reply came pronto, proving he wasn't sleeping, either. "I've *seen* her, but we're not together if that's what you're asking..."

"And by that, you mean not *yet*..."

"She's asked me for space, and I'm giving it to her."

"Real smooth, brother!"

Scott heard his brother shift position in the darkness.

"Instead of mourning the girl who doesn't love you anymore," David said, "why don't you concentrate on the one who's been in love with you all along?"

"What girl? What are you talking about?"

"Oh, you know. Tall, blonde, big blue eyes."

Scott stared at his brother's dark silhouette, puzzled. "Who?"

"Barbie librarian—does it ring a bell? Yes? No?"

"You mean Madison? She isn't in love with me, we're just friends."

"Gosh, you're even dumber than I thought," David said mockingly. "Trust me, the girl's a goner for you."

"You know what? I'm sleeping on the couch."

Without another word, Scott grabbed his pillow and comforter and headed downstairs. As he stared at the living room ceiling, he found he wasn't able to shake David's words off. Visions of blue eyes and blond hair kept swiping before his eyes. Her kind smile and cute freckles… Madison, in love with him? Was it possible? And, finally, one question above all the others…

Do I want it to be true?

***

The next morning, once everyone had cleared the kitchen after breakfast, Scott stayed behind to help his mother with the preparations for the Christmas meal. It was their special "thing," and Scott had missed the tradition last year. It had seemed worth it at the time, because he'd met Haley in Hawaii, but now the entire past year felt like such a waste.

"And how have you been doing?" his mom asked after a while.

He shrugged while peeling potatoes for the mash—she'd yet to promote him to more noble tasks like the stuffing of the turkey or the glazing of the ham. "I'm great, thanks."

"So is everything okay between you and your brother?"

"Yeah, sure."

"Is that why you slept on the couch last night?"

Busted.

He'd gone back to their room before anyone in the house had woken up, and he thought he'd gotten away with it. But nothing escaped his mother.

Scott kept quiet, so his mom continued. "I couldn't help but notice you seem subdued, while your brother is trying hard to pretend he's not out-of-his-mind-happy."

Damn, the woman had superpowers.

"Am I getting close?" she asked. And when Scott still said nothing, she insisted, "Is it a girl again?"

Scott startled at that. "What do you mean *again?*"

"Oh, Scott, please. You think I'm such an idiot I can't read my own two sons? It's like David's high school senior year all over again… Only the roles are reversed this time. He's on cloud nine, and you're pissed. Did David do something?"

"David…" Scott desperately wanted to say 'yes.' But other than coming onto Haley, David had done nothing entirely shady. He'd made it very clear he wanted her and would do everything he could to get the girl. And as much as Scott sought to blame his brother for sending him to California, the truth was he'd wanted to go. And if all it took for Haley to stop loving him was for David to woo her, then maybe it was better they'd broken up now.

Scott knew all of this *in theory*. But still, he couldn't control the suffocating pain in his throat whenever he thought of her, or the sensation of his heart being ripped out of his chest whenever he imagined her with his brother. "He's always been very upfront about how he felt for Haley."

"Are we talking about the brunette I met at the hospital?"

Scott nodded.

"So you've broken up?"

"Yep."

"And now she's with David?"

"It's only a matter of time."

Scott couldn't anticipate what his reaction would be when it happened for real. As much as he hated himself for it, hearing David say they were not together yet had left him so relieved.

"She seemed like a lovely girl," his mom continued. "But I'm sure there are plenty of other girls out there who'd be more than happy to go out with you."

Madison's face flashed before his eyes, but he shook the idea away. He wasn't going to let David play mind games with him.

"Maybe," Scott conceded. "But right now it all seems pointless."

"Give it time," his mom said, and steered him around to hug him. "It'll get better, I promise."

Scott let himself be cuddled, marveling at how such a tiny woman was able to dispense so much comfort.

After some rocking and gentle shoulder-patting, his mom sniffled and pushed back, saying, "Now, back to your peeling, you slacker. This dinner won't prepare itself."

Seventeen

Madison

On Christmas Day, Madison and her parents arrived at the family's country house in the early afternoon. The official dinner wouldn't start until five, but it was tradition for the Smithson clan to gather ahead of time and chat while nibbling snacks—accompanied by bubbly, thank goodness—and to exchange presents before the main meal.

Everyone was there: Vicky and her husband Robert, Ethan and Rose, a very pregnant Georgiana with Tyler, her aunt and uncle, her grandparents, and Uncle Frank—who wasn't exactly a relative, but who participated in all family gatherings. He always ended up drunk and asleep sooner rather than later.

Madison sat on an armchair strategically positioned so that her grandparents' giant Christmas tree would shield her from her father's view. She sank deep into the plush cushions and observed the rest of her family in silence, trying to avoid meeting anyone's eye.

Ethan, Vicky, and Rose were at the top of her no-eye-contact list. The three people who'd found her making out with Georgiana's husband on her wedding day. Each seemed to regard her with either patronizing or disheartening attitudes. Rose was all kind smiles, and Madison appreciated Ethan's girlfriend for the effort, but couldn't help registering the lingering pity behind her dark eyes. As for Ethan himself, Madison didn't dare look at him at all; he loved his sisters and was super protective of them, meaning that by extension he had to hate her. Vicky was the nicest, as usual, but still, Madison felt like blushing whenever their gazes crossed.

Then she had to avoid Georgiana for the exact opposite reason. "Gigi" didn't know about what had happened on her wedding day, and Madison dreaded her cousin would find out just by glimpsing into her guilty eyes. And even if that fear was absurd, it was wise to leave Georgiana alone under any circumstances. She was invariably nasty to Madison, and now that she was pumped full of estrogen, who knew to what new extremes she could go.

And then there was Tyler, who Madison had to avoid at all cost for obvious reasons.

Ah, and her father, who had just vowed a few hours ago to never speak to her again. Thinking about it, that could actually be a huge improvement. Better he never spoke to her again, rather than yell at her nonstop for being stupid, naïve, a hopeless dreamer, or regale her with the shouted version of the whole "if you want to live the life of a starving artist be my guest, but don't expect to have access to my money while you play around with your stories instead of living in the real world" sermon.

Yep. Her father hadn't taken well the news of her refusal to apply to law school. And, true to expectations, he'd skipped the cajoling and bribing phases altogether to jump right into the classic Smithson-angry-dad-who-blackmails-his-kids-with-money power play.

So Madison sat in silence in her chair, drinking more wine than she ate food, and watching the "Georgiana Show." Her cousin was only ten days away from her due date and was talking about everything ranging from labor horror stories and delivery room breathing techniques, to diaper changing best practices, to a painfully detailed account of the nanny auditions she'd held so far.

When she couldn't stomach any more of it, Madison grabbed another flute of champagne and escaped to the veranda to have a moment alone. It was dark in here, the only illumination coming from the fairy lights strung all around the house and the bluish snow-reflected glow of the garden. At four thirty in the afternoon, it was already night time. But, between natural and artificial lights, her grandparents' garden was well lit, and Madison could admire its snowy outline. Outdoor furniture, shrubs, flowerbeds, the pool… everything was covered in a thick coat of dusty snow, leaving only the silhouettes of what was lying underneath. If it kept on snowing, soon nothing would be recognizable anymore. The garden would transform into a white desert, with dunes and slopes forged by the strong wind that had been blowing on the outskirts of Boston since last week.

A shiver crept down her spine; it was colder here on the veranda. The thick glass enclosing the room was not enough to keep out the freezing cold that was attacking the entirety of Northern America. Madison grabbed a blanket, wrapped it around her shoulders, and kept on staring out of the glass walls while sipping champagne.

She was still contemplating the snow when the sound of footsteps startled her. Turning around, she was surprised to find herself staring into Ethan's cold blue eyes. They held each other's stare for an instant before Madison lowered her gaze to the floor, already blushing in embarrassment.

"Oh," Ethan said. "I didn't think anyone would be here. I needed a moment alone."

"I'll get out of your way," Madison promptly replied, dropping the blanket back on the couch and making a quick dash for the door.

But Ethan grabbed her by the elbow before she'd cleared it. "Hey, you don't have to go."

Now she was forced to hold his gaze, and she could read only disgust in his eyes. "Please, Ethan, no need to pretend. I know Vicky gave you the be-nice-to-your-damaged-cousin speech, but she isn't here… so no need to pretend, really."

Ethan arched his brows. "What's that supposed to mean?"

"I see the way you cringe every time you're around me. So let's just avoid each other and not make this any more awkward than it needs to be."

Instead of letting her go, Ethan gently grabbed her by the shoulders. "Madison, I'm not mad at you. I mean, if I can stand to sit down at dinner with that prick my sister married—"

"See, Ethan, that's the problem. I don't want anyone in my family to have to stand my presence." She shrugged free of his grip. "So I'll just go."

Ethan, however, didn't seem so ready to let her go. He jumped backward and blocked her path to the door, saying, "That came out wrong. I'm not mad at you…"

Madison just narrowed her eyes at him.

"I know I scowl at you sometimes; Rose already chided me on that. But it's because looking at you reminds me of what happened that day, and I get mad whenever I remember my sister is married to such a"—he growled, and flared his nostrils—"Anyway, Madison, we're family. One mistake, or even a thousand mistakes, couldn't change that."

Madison swallowed, all choked up. "Really?"

"Come here." Ethan pulled her into a tight hug. "Is this why you're hiding out here?"

"Yes, and no." Madison sniffled, pulling back. "It's mostly my dad."

"Why? What did Uncle John do?"

Madison studied Ethan for a second before replying. Well, if there was another person in the family who could understand her, it was the other non-lawyer black sheep of the flock. So Madison opened up to him. "I told him I'm not applying to law school, and he didn't take it well."

Ethan let out a low whistle.

"You're the only other Smithson to turn down the Smithson *Legacy*," Madison said sarcastically. "Does it get better in time?"

"Me? I'm a pathetic loser compared to you. I went through the ropes of going to law school, passing the bar, and living the miserable life of a corporate lawyer for a whole year before I found the guts to say enough. You're a rock star."

"Yeah, but you were the first to rebel. Was it worth it?"

"Totally." Ethan became super serious. "Madison, if you're sure you don't want to be a lawyer, believe me, it's a thousand times better that you've said so right away. You can't force yourself to change. Trust me, I tried, and it didn't work. I became more miserable with every passing day until I exploded and had to call it quits. This way you save four or five painful years of life no one could ever give back to you. And Uncle John will come round. You're his only daughter."

"Which only makes it worse." Madison chewed on her bottom lip. "At least your father had spares. Vicky is already in the company, and Georgiana may join when the baby is old enough, but I'm an only child. If I don't join Smithson and Smithson, our side of the family is out, full stop."

"That's not true. Uncle John doesn't have to sell his partnership, and if your kids want to become lawyers, they'll always have a place there."

My kids? Madison scoffed inside her head. *Assuming I don't die a spinster.*

"But Smithson and Smithson is our fathers' dream," Ethan continued, "not ours. And it's not fair of them to expect us to give up our dreams for theirs."

"So I made the right choice?"

"One hundred percent. I'm not saying it'll be easy, but you're saving yourself a lot of grief by ripping the Band-Aid now. Did the threats already start?"

"Yep. I'm cut-off from his money. Whatever that means."

"At the worst, it means paying back your tuition. Do you already have a plan in mind?"

"He hasn't asked for anything yet, but he's promised to cancel all my credit cards. Anyway, I can apply for a student loan to finish the year, and I hope I'll manage next year by cutting back a little."

"You know what you'll do once you graduate? I mean, I'm here if you ever need help, financially or otherwise."

"Let's hope that won't be necessary. They offered me a scholarship for grad school for a research project I'm working on, and one of my professors wants me to be a TA." She smiled and shrugged. "Anyway, if things take a turn for the worse, I can always sell the car."

"Damn, our fathers are real assholes." Ethan wrapped an arm around Madison's shoulders and steered her toward the door. "Let's go pretend to be one big happy family, if only for Grandma's sake."

"Hey." Madison turned her head to look up at him. "You never told me why you came to hide out here?"

Ethan flashed her a wicked smile. "Oh, that. I'm about to do something very stupid, and I just told Grandma, meaning I can't change my mind now." It was clear from his tone that Ethan wasn't going to elaborate further, so Madison followed him to the dining room, wondering what in hell he could possibly mean by "something very stupid."

***

They were just past the appetizers when Georgiana dropped her fork with a loud clattering of silver on porcelain and let out a pitiful whimper.

"Are you okay?" Almost everyone around the table asked a variation of the question at the same time.

Georgiana stood extra still for a few seconds, and finally smiled. "False alarm. It was a small cramp, but nothing serious."

The other thirteen people at the table, Madison included, let out a collective sigh of relief, and the first course was served. From that moment on, however, Madison couldn't help noticing Tyler watching Georgiana as if she were a time bomb, being extra attentive to her cousin's every movement. Especially since Georgiana kept wincing as if in pain from time to time. Until the winces became full grimaces of pain, and Georgiana grabbed her belly and groaned.

Once again, every head at the table turned

toward Georgiana, who grimaced again and announced, "I think the baby wants out."

She might as well have shouted, *"Ready, steady, GO!"* because at once everyone dropped glasses, cutlery, bread… whatever it was they had in their hands, and jumped up from the table shouting orders or asking questions.

"We need to drive to the hospital." Georgiana's mom.

"Did you bring your bag?" Tyler.

"I'm getting the car." Both Ethan and his dad.

"Ahhh, it hurts." Georgiana.

"Deep breaths." Vicky.

"Oh, dear." Grandma. "A new baby on Christmas Day."

"Someone get her coat." Madison's father.

"It reeeeah-haaally hurts." Georgiana again.

In a coat-grabbing rush, everyone was up and moving across the hall to get to the front door. Georgiana was supported by her mom and sister, as she suddenly seemed in too much pain to walk on her own. It was amidst all the frenzy that Ethan rushed back to his chair, unceremoniously yanked his jacket from the back of the seat, and made the world stop for a few seconds.

Everyone in the room—Georgiana included—froze to watch a small, velvety red box fly out of his jacket's pocket in a wide arc and land on the living room rug. It popped open to reveal a white gold ring with a single, square-cut diamond set on top.

Rose stared at the tiny box, transfixed. Her hands moved up to cover her mouth. Then she looked at Ethan with tears already welling in her eyes.

"Well…" Ethan smiled oh-so-charmingly with his devil-may-care attitude. "That's not how I intended to do it, but since we're here." He got down on one knee to retrieve the red box and then, turning it toward Rose, he asked, "Rose, will you marry me?"

The entire room waited in silence for Rose's answer. Even Georgiana made an effort not to scream through what must've been a really painful contraction, judging by how she scrunched up her face and bit her lower lip, struggling not to cry out.

"Yes," Rose said, tears running down her cheeks. "Yes, yes, yes."

She knelt in front of Ethan and kissed him for a long moment, before letting go and allowing him to slide the beautiful ring on her finger. Madison realized it was Grandma's ring—that must've been the very stupid thing Ethan had referred to earlier: he'd asked their grandmother for the ring.

Cheers and claps erupted all around and were promptly interrupted by an inhuman scream coming from Georgiana. "Can we get a move on, people?" she yelled. "I'm kinda having a baby here!"

So it was that the Smithson family spent Christmas Day in a waiting room at Massachusetts General Hospital, and that, at 11:49 p.m., the beautiful Jane Smithson Bronfam came into the world as a screaming, healthy baby girl of seven and a half pounds.

Eighteen

Haley

Haley was in the kitchen with her mom, spending Boxing Day afternoon doing a sweet nothing after the eating marathon that had been Christmas Day. They'd even allowed her dad some diet leeway, and with everyone in a joyful, festive mood, the celebration had passed in a vortex of cheers, good food, family anecdotes, and present unwrapping.

Like many of her fellow students, Haley had the impression the entire month of December had slipped through her fingers in a heartbeat. She'd taken a long breath at the end of the term, to then survive in a revising-exam-taking apnea for twenty days and then, boom, boom, boom: pack, go home, and finish all the last minute Christmas shopping until the twenty-fifth finally arrived. And today, with the holiday behind her, was the first essentially calm day of the month. Which, unfortunately, meant she'd had plenty of time to think.

She would've liked to sleep in late, but no, she'd found herself staring wide-eyed at the ceiling at dawn, unable to shake off the fact that no one special had wished her a merry Christmas.

Next, she'd wondered who she wanted that someone special to be. Blue sparkly eyes and a crooked grin had appeared in answer. *David.*

Haley hadn't been surprised at how clear a reply her subconscious had provided. In the one and a half months since the breakup, she'd been taken aback by how easily her life had kept going. No tears, no desperation, no sense of hopelessness. The only explanation she could give herself had been that the real mourning phase of her relationship with Scott had passed during the summer. When she'd had to learn day by painful day not to rely on him, not to see him, not to talk to him… and also when she'd started falling out of love with him…

Ironically, she'd sort of hoped to be heartbroken. A part of her still couldn't believe she was letting go of such a great guy. One stubborn piece of her heart couldn't reconcile with not having any more feelings for a boy she'd fallen so hard for. But that was the reality of it.

The only thing that made Haley's heart beat these days were memories of little moments she'd had with David. She'd walk around with a silly, secret smile stamped on her lips after remembering something David had said, or a cute face he'd pulled, or his concentrated frown while he tried to solve a difficult problem… And more than once, she'd cursed herself for not kissing him the day he'd waited for her after class. The echo of his whispered words in her ear when he hadn't kissed her—*"Pity I have to give you space."*—was enough for her to break out in an all-body case of goosebumps.

"Oh!" Her mom gasped, stopping dead in front of the kitchen's window and yanking Haley out of her introspective moment.

Haley wiped another one of her secret smiles from her lips and, dipping a cookie into her tea, she asked, "What's up?"

"Nothing, really." Her mom shrugged the question off. "The neighbors are… mmm… building a weird-looking snowman."

"Something worth seeing?"

"*No!* No. I mean, not really."

Miranda moved away from the window and took the stool next to Haley, looking pensive. She sat quietly for a while. Then, out of the blue, she asked, "I couldn't help but notice the lack of text messaging and late-night calls. Is everything all right, honey?"

Haley guessed she must tell her sooner or later. Even though she spoke to her parents twice a week during the school year, she was very private when it came to her romantic life, and hadn't told them about the breakup yet.

"Scott and I broke up."

"Mmm…" Atypically, her mom didn't say

'sorry' or offer words of comfort. She only asked, "Why?"

"I'd really rather not talk about it."

"Was it because of the brother?"

Ah, mothers! They were a dreadful species.

"Mom, I'm serious, not now."

Even more peculiarly, her mom didn't insist. Instead, she came out with, "You should go for a walk outside."

"Are you delirious? It's thirty degrees out there, and I'm drinking tea."

"I'll make you another one later," she said, grabbing Haley's mug and emptying it into the sink.

"Hey," Haley protested. "I was drinking that."

"Oh, hush, the sun is shining and it's a beautiful day." To Haley's utter dismay, her mom started pushing her out of the kitchen. "Out, out… you're too young to stay shut in here and drink tea all afternoon like an old lady."

Okay, something was definitely up with her mom. This was highly unusual behavior. Haley was not in the mood to deal with mommy-strangeness right then, so she donned her coat, beanie, scarf, and Ugg boots, and headed outside just to shut the woman up.

Haley stepped out onto the porch, scanning the neighborhood to decide if she should head right or left. She froze in surprise when she spotted a familiar face leaning against a familiar midnight blue truck, waiting for her.

Her heart skipped a beat.

At that moment, she felt like Molly Ringwald in the final scene of *Sixteen Candles*—minus the eighties bridesmaid dress and warm weather. Just like Jake Ryan in the movie, David was staring up at her with a small grin on his handsome face. Haley could almost hear the notes of *If You Were Here* by the Thompson Twins as she hopped down the steps of her parents' front porch with the same shy anticipation as an insecure sixteen-year-old Sam Baker.

"Hi," she said.

He watched her approach. "Hi."

"What are you doing here?"

"I figured you've had enough space."

Judging from the tight pull she'd felt in her chest when she'd spotted him standing outside her home, he was right. She stepped closer. "You must be freezing, waiting out here," she said softly.

He gestured to his truck. "I've only been waiting for about a minute. I got out of my car when I saw your mother waving at me and giving me the thumbs up... I figured you'd come out soon enough."

Haley turned her head over her shoulder to check the kitchen window. There was a rustling of curtains and then nothing else, as if someone had been spying and now was gone.

Mothers! Really, an impossible breed.

"Can we talk?" David asked.

Haley nodded, and walked around and slid into the passenger's side. David climbed into the driver's seat, his long legs and tall frame filling the space next to her.

He started the truck and turned on the heat—even though the inside was still warm—leaving the gear in Park.

"Let's go somewhere, please?" Haley asked.

As much as she was eager to hear what David had to say, she didn't want to do so within reach of her mother's prying eyes.

David smiled and switched the truck into Drive. "You're the expert; tell me where to go."

She guided him to a small park just around the corner from her house. It usually wasn't that scenic a sight, but in winter, coated in snow, with ice crystals as natural decorations, and blue fairy lights wrapped around the various tree trunks, it gained a romantic winter-wonderland vibe.

David parked in the deserted lot and left the car on, warm air blasting all around them from the vents.

Haley angled herself in the seat toward him, unwrapping the scarf from around her neck just to have something to do with her hands. "So? Why are you here?"

Without saying a word, he raised his hand to cup her cheek and leaned forward to kiss her. A long, deep kiss.

"I'm done waiting," he said when he pulled back.

Fair enough. Now that they were together, so close in the confined space of his truck, Haley was done waiting, too. The test was over. She didn't miss Scott. He already felt like a distant memory, and she couldn't believe she'd ever thought of Scott as "the one" because it all paled compared to what she was feeling now as she held David's deep blue gaze.

He ran a finger along her cheek, his voice soft but firm. "So what's it gonna be, Haley?"

She leaned in and kissed him again, sliding her arms around David's neck and pulling him closer until things got so heated that she forcefully had to pull away.

She slid her hands inside her coat and wrapped it more tightly around herself, not because she was cold, but because she was afraid that if she got her hands on David again, she wouldn't be able to pull back this time. "Where do we go from here?"

"I have to be back in Boston by the second— grad school sucks, and all." David rolled his eyes. "But we can go wherever you want for the next couple of days…"

"Any place in mind?"

"Doesn't matter. I'm not planning on letting you out of the room much."

Something melted in Haley's belly, and words failed her.

David winked and put his hands back on the wheel. "Let's get you home now. You need to pack."

Nineteen

Haley

Haley's parents didn't object to her early departure; especially not her mom, who confessed her secret membership to the #TeamDavid club. And after her dad had given David a thorough grilling on driving on ice, interspersed with not-so-subtle make-my-daughter-suffer-and-you'll-deal-with-me threats, they were good to go. The most obvious destination was to spend a few days at Niagara Falls State Park. The drive was only thirty minutes from Buffalo, and there were plenty of cozy and romantic cabin lodges not too far from the falls.

Reservations made, all they had to do was follow the GPS instructions which, after a long drive along the I-190 N, brought them to a less beaten, winding road.

"If I didn't know better," David commented, observing the forest-y surroundings, "I'd say you're taking me somewhere you'll be able to do as you please with me…"

Ah… well, yes, they'd be… pretty isolated.

"I figured this way we wouldn't have to remember that annoying 'do not disturb' sign."

David flashed her a wolfish smile, giving Haley's insides another good twist.

Will it ever stop? Haley wondered if he'd always have this effect on her. A part of her hoped he would, and the other was scared to death at that same possibility.

They drove around another few bends, until the road ended in a clearing at what appeared to be the main resort lodge. There were no other cars in the driveway, and the guy they'd talked to over the phone had seemed surprised they'd requested a cabin. These accommodations were more popular in the summer when it wasn't this freezing outside.

David parked in the spot with the least snow and, after hopping out of the truck, they headed for the small wooden house that must serve as reception.

"Ah, you're here already," a short man greeted them from behind the counter. Without wasting time, he grabbed a set of heavy-looking keys and a map and rounded the desk to give them the basic instructions. "You're in cabin eight. We weren't expecting anyone so close to Christmas. Usually, our winter guests prefer to come closer to New Year's Eve and stay only a couple of nights, but I have you down for six nights, correct?"

"Correct," David confirmed.

"With such short notice, we only just turned on

the heating in your cabin. It might take a while for the room to get to a decent temperature. But you're free to wait here as long as you like, and there's a fully functional fireplace in your bungalow already equipped with three days' worth of firewood."

"*Heat* won't be a problem," David said with such a straight face that Haley wondered if she was so randy she was reading double entendres into every innocent phrase. But then David sent her a wicked smile that gave her no doubt what he really meant. A shiver of anticipation ran down her spine.

"Very well," the clerk said, and proceeded to show them on the map how to get to their cabin. "We don't offer room service," he concluded. "But there's a convenience store two miles up the main road that's open 24/7, and of course all the restaurants in town. Please let me know if you'd like any recommendations."

"Great," David said, taking the map and keys.

"Again, if you need anything at all, call me. You have my number."

Within minutes they were back in the truck, cruising along an even smaller road surrounded by thick forest on both sides. Along the way, they passed a few other bungalow-style guest lodges, until they finally reached number eight: a tiny log cabin in the middle of the woods.

As the receptionist had predicted, the inside wasn't much warmer than the outside, and Haley eyed the fireplace as her last hope. The rest of the cabin was simple and very earthy, but with a modern-chic vibe. Everything was made of wood: roof, walls, floor, furniture…

The layout was pretty basic: an open space with a small kitchenette and dining area on one side, a large space in front of the fireplace covered by a giant white rug of several sheep skins joined together, a door to the side that must lead to the bathroom, and a giant king-sized bed at the back of the room. Haley's eyes lingered on the bed longer than on everything else.

Coming in, David didn't seem concerned by the low temperature. He closed the door behind them, set their bags near the bed, rather business-like, and removed his coat so he could work on building up a fire. Haley watched, impressed, as he crumpled a few newspaper pages into paper balls, threw them into the fire pit, and started building an orderly pyramid of progressively thicker logs.

She sat on the rug in front of the fire, not removing her coat or any of her cold weather accessories. Hat, scarf, gloves… she kept everything on. "I never knew you had such a handy side," she teased.

He peeked at her over his shoulder, a

dangerous promise in his eyes. "There's still much you don't know about me."

I'm sure we're going to close the gap tonight, Haley thought, swallowing.

Once the fire was up and burning, David settled on the rug next to her. "Still cold?" he asked.

"Not so much…"

She made to remove her beanie, but David caught her wrist midair. "Let me."

He knelt in front of her and, moving tortuously slowly, pulled off her hat. Then he gently unwrapped the scarf from around her neck, and pulled off her gloves, one first, then the other, his eyes never leaving hers. The buttons of her coat were his next victim and, once he was done, he pushed it off her shoulders. The boots went next, followed by her socks. As he pulled her sweater over her head, he paused to look at her for a few long moments, as if he needed to etch every second into his mind. She used the pause to sneak her hands under his sweater and lift it up. Ever the collaborative, David tugged it off his back in one fluid motion and discarded it next to the mounting pile of her clothes.

Then his lips were on hers, all restraint finally gone. He laid her backward on the rug and climbed on top of her, careful to keep his weight on his elbows. As they kissed, other useless clothes were shed. When they were down to only their underwear, he stopped again. David looked at her with such burning intensity that Haley was overwhelmed by the strength of her feelings; *their* feelings.

"I love you."

Haley reached up to cup his face. "I think I do more than love you…"

David smiled down at her. "What's that supposed to mean?"

"That I've never felt something so…" *Strong, intense, overpowering…* no word seemed big enough. "So…"

"Shhh…" He pressed a finger to her lips. "I know…"

He leaned down and kissed her again, and again, and again. And as they made love for the first time, there was no more need to talk… their eyes spoke for them. And their lips, and their hands, and their bodies…

***

"I like that face," Haley said, rolling over in bed to place her chin on David's naked chest. After a long time spent on the rug the night before, they'd finally moved to the bed.

"What face?" David asked.

"Relaxed, unguarded… serene."

"I'm happy."

"And I'm starving," Haley said, sliding out of bed and regaling David with a full view of her naked rear side. "How about breakfast?"

"You can't ask me about breakfast looking like that," David protested.

"Well, sorry, but I really am starving."

Haley moved next to the fireplace to put on yesterday's clothes, and she was just pulling up the zipper of her jeans when David grabbed her from behind. Shifting the hair away from her neck, he started trailing kisses from right below her ear down to her collarbone. "Are you sure I can't interest you in a rematch?"

Haley laughed and wriggled away. She bent to get her sweater, and picked up David's clothes, too, pushing them into his hands. "Clothes on. You're treating me to breakfast." She watched him obediently put his pants and shirt on, and then, with a coquettish smile, she added, "Also, we might want to stock up a little, just in case we don't feel like going out much in the next few days."

David's eyes darkened. He pulled her close and whispered, "You're right, we need to stock up."

***

On the first day of the new year, Haley and David were all packed and ready to get back to the real world. They'd played house for six amazing days, cooking meals, making love, building a snowman, making love, going on cozy restaurant dates, making love… They'd even ventured out of the cabin to visit the frozen-over falls. But now it was time to return to Boston, and time for a big reality check. As much as Haley loved it, they couldn't live in a bubble forever.

"You got everything?" David asked, scanning the room for any forgotten items.

"Yeah. Listen, David, before we go, we need to…"

"No. No, no, no." David pushed a finger on her lips. "Don't…"

Haley pulled his hand aside, interlocking their fingers. "You don't even know what I want to say."

"No, but I'm assuming it starts with 'What happens when we're back in Boston?' and ends with 'We need to tell Scott.'"

"He should know."

"Not right away."

"He already knows there's something between us. I mean, it's the reason he and I broke up. Didn't you talk at all when you were at home?"

"Yeah, he asked me if we were together."

"And what did you say?"

"I said 'no' because at the time we weren't together."

"All the more reason to come clean."

David took his phone out of his pocket. "So, what? You want me to call him now and tell him?"

"Not over the phone. But as soon as we get back to Boston we're going to tell him, okay?"

David shrugged. "I hope you'll still like me with a black eye or two."

Haley smiled and cupped his cheek. "Even with a broken nose." She rose on tiptoes to kiss him.

"I see you've mastered the carrot and stick thing," David joked after the kiss.

"Is it working?"

"Like a charm." David pressed his lips to her forehead. "Listen, the Crimson have an away game against Vermont tomorrow. We'll tell him when he comes back... And tonight... we can have another selfish night all to ourselves..." He gave her a long kiss.

Haley kept her arms wrapped around him after breaking the kiss. "And I'm supposed to be the expert on the carrot and stick thingy, huh?"

David smirked. "Shall we?"

Holding hands, they exited the cabin and got in the truck, ready for the long drive home.

***

After being gone from her apartment for a good ten days, Haley needed a serious round of grocery shopping. She'd spent two nights at David's place and hadn't had any time to go to the supermarket until now. Plus, she needed to busy herself with something mundane, not to think about how tonight was the night David would tell Scott about their relationship. They'd debated for a long time if they should tell him together, but Haley had suggested David do it alone. They were brothers, and they needed to work out their issues.

Haley was pushing her cart through the cereal aisle when she spotted a familiar figure a few feet ahead of her. She froze, undecided on what to do, just as Scott turned and their eyes met. The initial look of surprise on his face was quickly replaced by a mix of hurt and contempt. He held her gaze for a few impossibly long seconds. Then, without a single word or nod of acknowledgment, he walked away.

Well, then.

"Scott," she called. "Wait."

Haley left her cart behind to run after him. "Are we at the point we can't even say hello to each other?"

Scott stopped and turned to face her. "You're sleeping with my brother. Kind of puts a damper on things."

His words, cold with suppressed fury and lined

with harsh resentment, were like a slap in her face. "Scott, I'm… how…?"

"How do I know? Matt told me you spent the night at my old place. I assume it wasn't to play Scrabble. How convenient for you… all you had to do was switch doors."

Matt! They'd crossed paths for ten seconds on New Year's Day as he was leaving the house to go to Vermont, and neither Haley nor David had imagined he'd tell Scott.

"Scott, I'm sorry you found out that way. David wanted to be the one to tell you."

"Oh! Is that what the 'we need to talk' text was about? Well, you can tell him he can save his speech."

"I'm sorry."

"Well, so am I."

After another withering look, Scott dropped his grocery basket on the floor and stormed out of the supermarket without buying anything.

***

"He'll come round," David reassured her later that evening.

They were in his apartment, cuddling on his bed.

"I don't know, David, you should've seen his face. I think we really hurt him."

"He can survive, believe me. I did it for a year."

"It's different. I was never with you before."

"Didn't change the way I felt about you."

"Now you're just trying to sweet-talk me."

"What if I am?" He pushed a lock of hair away from her face. "Would it be so bad? Is it too selfish for me to want to enjoy this moment, just me and you, without worrying about anybody else's hurt feelings?"

"A little."

"Well, sorry to break it to you, but I'm selfish. I take what I want and do what I want… and right now the only thing I want is this…" He pressed his lips to hers, silencing any further protest she might've had.

Twenty

Scott

If nothing else, the discovery of Haley and David's relationship refocused Scott's anger on the basketball court. Where his fury had been pointless before, now he channeled his aggressiveness into a single aim: winning. He launched himself into one physical confrontation after another, his fear from the first game long gone. Almost as if now Scott *wanted* to get hurt.

The new style soon showed its consequences in an ever-growing number of faults being added to his box score, but also an outstanding tally of successful rebounds and blocked offensive actions. Coach Morrison didn't appear to mind the change much. As long as Scott kept it under the per-game fault limit, Morrison seemed fine giving him more leeway than his teammates. After all, he was supposed to be the muscle of the team.

So Scott poured all his efforts into basketball and training until winter recess was over and classes resumed, providing him with the added distraction of homework and his med school pre-application. Best way to keep his mind off things—off people.

And eventually, day by day, game by game, his heart started to mend. The part of him that had loved Haley, and then hated her, finally leaned toward a non-emotion closer to indifference. If he saw her in a supermarket now, he was sure he'd at least be able to complete his shopping without running away.

It was in this state of mind that Scott walked into his only literary class of the term, three whole weeks after finding out about Haley and David. He was early, so he took a seat at the almost empty table and waited for the other students and professor to show. He was busy staring into space, thinking about nothing, when someone said, "Hi" and took the chair on his right.

Madison.

Scott hadn't thought about her or what David had hinted at since Christmas, but now that she'd magically appeared next to him, he couldn't help but wonder…

"Hey," he said, looking her straight in the eyes.

They *were* big and of the deepest ocean blue.

She was beautiful, there was no denying it, and today she looked cute with her hair pinned in a messy bun by a yellow pencil, and with her librarian-style, extra-large glasses perched on her nose.

Madison held his gaze for barely half a second before looking away to take a notepad out of her school bag. A faint blush spread on her cheeks.

Mmm, interesting, Scott thought.

"So, how were the holidays?" Madison asked, clearly trying to appear nonchalant but still coming off flustered.

"My brother slept with my ex. Not my best Christmas."

"Oh." Madison covered her mouth with her hand, then lowered it to say. "I'm so sorry, I wasn't thinking…"

"Nah, it doesn't matter," Scott reassured her. "I've moved on."

"Really? How? I mean, good for you."

"I realized Haley and I were never a good fit, you know? We had so little in common…"

Madison stared at her blank notepad for a while, then asked, "So you're over her?"

Scott shrugged. "Getting there…"

"Great." Madison blushed again. "For you…"

"Hello, class." The professor walked in. "Welcome to the advanced fiction writing workshop. I know we all probably had a long day, and a four-to-seven lecture time is never ideal, but we all have to work with what we're given… so I'll keep the introduction brief. I'm Professor Mitchell." The instructor paused to write her name on the board. "And I'll be your teacher for the spring term…"

Everyone started jotting down notes—well,

everyone except for Madison, who was frantically searching for something. First, under her notepad, then in her bag, and even on the floor.

"This course will focus on the structure, execution, and revision of short fiction, with a longer project due for your final assignment…"

As Professor Mitchell kept going with her introduction, Scott whispered, "What are you looking for?"

"…throughout the whole term, we will read and discuss literary fiction from a craft perspective, concentrating on revision as well…"

"My pencil," Madison whispered back. "I can't find it."

"…the teaching approach will be primarily the discussion of student work…"

Scott leaned forward on his elbows. "You mean the one in your hair?"

"…with the aim of improving both writer-ly skills and critical analysis…"

Madison grasped at her messy bun, searching for the pencil. In one fluid motion, she freed it from its knot, sending a cascade of golden locks tumbling down her shoulders. Scott stared, mesmerized. At four in the afternoon, the sun was already setting and a warm orange glow was filtering through the window, hitting Madison's face with just the right light. Scott took in the halo of blond curls, her big blue eyes, and he also noted new details… like the cute little freckles that dotted her nose and cheeks. He frowned. How had he never noticed how beautiful she was?

"What's with the Heathcliff scowl?" Madison asked.

And she made literary quips, too.

"…Needless to say, *participation* is a key element of your final grade," the professor concluded, looking pointedly in their direction.

Scott threw Madison a so-busted, let's-be-model-students-from-now-on stare, and they spent the rest of the class in utter silence unless it was to say something course related.

***

After class, Scott and Madison made their way out of Baker Center together. Even if he'd had a super long day, and practice with the team was scheduled for an ungodly hour the next morning, Scott didn't feel like going home yet, so he went out on a limb and said, "Hey, you want to grab a bite?"

He wasn't sure what he was doing, and he didn't have a hit-on-Madison agenda. He was going with the flow, following his instincts, which told him being around Madison felt good. Plus, she was so cute when she blushed, just as she was doing now at his invitation. Scott was sure he had dinner in the bag, when she surprised him.

"Err... I would love to." Madison looked away, even more uncomfortable. "But I really can't."

"Oh, right," Scott said. "No, I mean..."

"It's not what you think..."

Scott tilted his head questioningly.

"This is really embarrassing, but I'm totally broke at the moment."

Definitely not the answer Scott had expected.

"Broke? How?"

"Actually, it's all your fault." Madison smiled. "Remember last summer, when you told me to follow my dreams?"

Scott's memory flashed back to the night they'd met on the street and walked to her house together. "To be a writer?" he asked.

"More not to be a lawyer." Madison sighed. "I told my dad I'm not applying to law school, and, in true Smithson fashion, he cut me off."

"That's awful."

"I know, but I'm his only child, and it's a hit for him to let his legacy within the firm go." Madison shrugged. "Anyway, I've applied for a student loan, but until it kicks in I can't afford dinner out..."

"That's not a problem. Dinner's on me."

There came the cute blush again. "No, I couldn't..."

"Come on, I still owe you big time for our last group project. You covered for me when I was out of it, and I never got to thank you. The least I can do is feed you…"

Madison stared at him, a new spark in her eyes. "When you put it like that… Where to?"

"Shake Shack?"

"Sounds perfect."

Madison

"What's with the dreamy face?" Alice asked the second Madison walked into the living room.

Madison checked the house to make sure Haley wasn't there, then said, "I might've gone on a non-date with Scott."

"Define non-date, please?"

"Oh, you know, a date that isn't really a date…"

Alice closed the textbook she was highlighting and stared at her with a puzzled expression.

"How can I explain it?" Madison took the chair in front of Alice at the long rectangular dining table the three of them often used to study. Books and papers could be spread out on it much more comfortably than on their respective smaller desks. "It's like, it starts out innocently enough:

two friends grabbing a bite together after a long afternoon class. And then, BAM, in the middle of dinner you suddenly realize you're on a date… sort of…"

Alice smiled. "So how did this non-date go?"

"It was just perfect, and…" Madison stopped and started chewing on her bottom lip.

"That's not exactly a perfect-date face," Alice noted.

"You think Haley will have a problem with it? Should I ask her first?"

"*Ask* her?"

"Yeah, I mean, am I breaking a girl code here? You know, like never date your friend's ex, or something?"

"Well, she didn't ask your permission to go out with David, did she?"

"No, true. But David and I never were in a serious relationship, while Haley and Scott dated for almost a year."

"And dumped him because she's in love with his brother. You're in the clear… I mean, if something is happening with you and Scott, you should definitely be upfront and tell her, but not in an asking-permission way."

"Right."

"So…" Alice leaned forward on her elbows. "Is something happening between you and Scott?"

Madison couldn't help but smile. "I'm not

sure… but he was different today. For the first time, it felt like he was seeing me as a woman and not, you know, a friend, a classmate, or Haley's roommate. I can't explain it in words, but something changed…"

Alice grabbed her hands across the table. "I'm so happy for you."

Seeing her friend's bright smile made Madison dial back a notch. "I don't want to get my hopes up too much. It's really nothing at the moment." Then a horrible thought crossed Madison's mind.

"What?" Alice asked.

"You think he's over Haley? He was pretty beaten up when they broke up."

Alice turned serious, too. "Hard one to call, but if he's being flirty with you…"

"So he wouldn't want to try to make Haley jealous by going out with me?"

"No, never… Why would you think that?"

Madison pulled her hands free and waved Alice off. "His brother did just that."

"Yeah, but that's David. Scott's a good guy… he'd never stoop so low."

"Mmm…" Madison stared at the fake wood-grain of the table, tracing its curls with a finger.

"Madison." Alice knocked on the table to make her look up. "Scott is nothing like that, I promise."

"It doesn't matter, really. I'm probably

building castles in the air… I'm sure Scott saw tonight only as dinner with a friend."

"Hey," Alice said with a devilish smirk. "Want me to do some investigative work?"

"What do you mean?"

"We could ask Jack…"

"No, no… Already too many people know how I feel about Scott. I don't want Jack to know, too."

"Err…" Alice cleared her throat.

Madison gasped. "You already told him!"

"I might've said something a while ago. But don't worry, Jack is like a tomb. He won't say anything."

"But they live together!"

"Which is why we can ask him if Scott seems to be in a good mood. I mean, if he walked into the house with a smile matching yours, you have your answer."

The idea was too appealing for Madison to refuse, so she nodded.

Alice grabbed her phone and beckoned Madison to come sit next to her. Madison rounded the table, and they bent their heads together as Alice typed.

But you have to
be super stealthy

Dots appeared over Jack's name in the chat until
his reply came in.

Okay?

Is Scott home?

Yes?

How does he
seem?

What do you
mean?

Is he acting
strange?

Mmm... Sort of

Meaning?

He's whistling
under his breath

Ask him how his
day went

Do I have to call
him honey?

No, smartass... :)

Just ask him
about his day,
please?

The chat stood blank for a while until Jack's answer finally came in.

Says it's been his
best day in a long
while

Alice and Madison looked away from the chat and up at each other, both sporting cheeks-aching smiles.

251

Twenty-one
Scott

After a lot of cajoling, Scott convinced Madison to let him buy her dinner the next Wednesday, and the next. He was already working out a strategy to make her say 'yes' to a repeat tonight when she surprised him.

"So," Madison said as they exited Baker Center. "Where can I take you to dinner tonight?"

"You're taking me out?"

"Yes." She smiled coyly.

Scott studied her. "Your student loan kicked in?"

"Better than that... my mother kicked in."

She made a suspenseful pause, and Scott waited for her to elaborate.

"She told my dad that if he was free to make my last year in college a nightmare and force me to take on student debt, she was free to have him sleep on the couch." Madison smirked. "I don't think he made it past the first night."

Scott low-whistled.

"So now I'm back on a drastically reduced allowance, and I can treat you to a grand dinner a la tacos and fries... You in for Mexican?"

"Mexican sounds perfect."

***

Much later, when the check arrived, both Madison and Scott reached for it.

"Hey," Madison protested. "I said dinner was on me."

"Are you one of those feminists who never let men pay on a date?"

"If this were a date, I might let you pay."

Scott held onto the leather folder tight as he stared into Madison's blue eyes. "So let me pay…"

The blush that ensued had to be the fiercest yet. Madison let go of the folder and settled back in her seat, lowering her gaze. Scott slipped a few bills in, and they walked out of the restaurant without saying another word.

They'd been walking for a full block when Madison surprised him with a direct question. "So this was a date?" she asked, steadily looking at the curb.

Scott opted for an equally daring answer. "I'd like it to be."

"Why? I mean, you've never…" Madison stumbled over her words. "What changed?"

"I had a bit of an eye-opener," Scott confessed.

Madison stopped walking and turned to face him, bolder than he'd ever seen her. "What does that mean?"

Scott smirked teasingly. "David might've mentioned something over Christmas break…"

Now, this had to be the best, neck-to-forehead tomato red face ever. Her eyes were open wide and her mouth formed the cutest, shocked little 'O' shape.

"What did he say?"

Scott shrugged. "He hinted a beautiful, smart girl might have feelings for me."

Madison groaned. "Now I want to kill your brother."

Scott chuckled. "Welcome to the club."

A smile lit up Madison's face. Then the rest of what he'd said seemed to register in her eyes, and she turned serious again. "You think I'm beautiful?"

Scott stepped closer, pushing her long curls behind her ears and cupping her cheeks. "Very." Then he leaned in and kissed her. Madison kept still at first, too shy or too shocked to move. But after a few moments, she responded to the kiss with a passion Scott had not expected. Not that he was complaining.

After the kiss, he walked her home, both of them maintaining an embarrassed silence. When they stopped in front of her building, Scott wasted no more time with shyness. "Can I hope for a second date?" he asked.

Madison blushed and nodded.

"I have two home games this weekend against Columbia and Cornell, but I'm free Saturday morning. Want to grab a coffee?"

"Yes," Madison replied in a whisper.

Scott pulled her closer and gave her a soft kiss on the lips. "Until then…"

Madison

For their official second date, as two certified book-worms, Madison and Scott went to a reading from an author they both loved in downtown Boston. Afterward, they stopped to have coffee in a quaint, one-of-a-kind coffee shop near the bookstore. There were a lot more kisses involved, and Madison found herself unable to stop smiling. Not even when, later that evening, she had to get ready to go watch the Crimson play. Her almost non-existent love for the game rekindled at once.

"Maddie, are you ready?" Alice called from the hall.

"Just a second!" Madison shouted back. "I'll be right there."

Haley hadn't come to a basketball match since game one of the season, back at the beginning of November, but Madison had kept going to keep Alice company. And, yes, also to watch Scott play. But tonight was the first night she officially had a reason to go: Scott had asked her.

Madison fluffed her hair in front of the mirror and was about to exit her bedroom when she overheard Alice and Haley talking on the other side of the door.

"Are you sure you'll be okay at home all by yourself?" Alice asked.

"Yeah, I have tons of homework to do," Haley reassured her.

"Is David coming over?"

"No, he's going to the game."

"Oh." Alice sounded surprised. "So why don't you come, too?"

"I don't want Scott to see me there."

Madison's heart sank. Did Haley believe Scott still had feelings for her?

Thankfully, Alice asked the very same question. "But he's moved on from you. So what's the issue?"

"From me, yes, but not from what happened with his brother. They were still bickering over Brigitte after they'd both been over the girl forever. I want to give them space. They're brothers… they have their issues, but deep down they love each other. They just have to stop being so damn stubborn…"

Madison sighed with relief. On Wednesday night, when she'd come back home after Scott had kissed her, she'd waited a reasonable amount of time to allow herself to become stable and coherent enough, and then she'd knocked on Haley's door to tell her. The conversation had been pretty smooth. Madison had told Haley about the kiss, and her friend, after a moment of shock, had wished her and Scott to be happy, saying neither of them could hope to find a better person. Madison was relieved to know now that Haley had been sincere.

Yes, the situation would still be strange for a while, but Madison hoped that, in time, the we-both-dated-the-other-brother-first awkwardness would go away.

"Madison," Alice called again. "We're going to be late."

With a deep breath, Madison opened the door. "You can stop yelling. I'm here."

***

Just as they were about to get seated at Lavietes Pavilion, someone grabbed Madison from behind and gently pushed her one seat over.

"This is my seat, Blondie," David said, sitting on the chair between her and Alice.

Madison glared at him.

"Whoa, what's with the smoldering look?"

"I'm not talking to you," Madison said,

crossing her arms over her chest and stubbornly looking away.

"May I ask why?"

Madison turned, pointing a finger at him. "You told Scott I had feelings for him when you promised you'd never do that. I'm *so* mad at you."

"Mmm, interesting, because last I heard, my little slip of the tongue sent my brother flying right into your open arms."

Madison opened her mouth to argue but found herself at a loss for sarcastic retorts.

"So." David smiled, as cocksure as ever. "What you really mean by 'mad' is how grateful you are I've knocked some sense into my brother's head, right?"

With Haley's words fresh in her mind, Madison asked, "So, how are things with you and Scott?"

"Oh." David shrugged. "He knows he owes me."

"Owes you?"

"Yeah. If it weren't for me, he would've said 'no' to California, and now he wouldn't be dating the only girl right for him."

Alice scoffed on David's other side. "Oh, gosh, you *are* smooth."

"You have a problem with me, too?"

"As long as you keep my best friend happy, no, I don't."

David stretched in his chair like a cat. "Glad we can all be one happy family." Then he nudged Madison's shoulder. "Come on, Blondie, away with the scowl. You know you can't stay mad at me…"

Madison's lips twitched, and she rolled her eyes. The dude really was impossible.

"Friends?" David asked, and she nodded.

"Friends."

Just then the referee whistled, and all eyes turned to the game. Madison shouted in encouragement. Finally, she could cheer for the boy she loved with no need to hold back…

***

Madison had to wait another three days to see Scott again. Between conflicting class schedules, his basketball practice sessions plus biweekly games, and her book club, it was difficult for them to find a quiet moment to meet. So, Wednesday nights had become their fixed date amidst the chaos of the rest of the week. They'd spend three good hours eye flirting in class, then go out to dinner together. Or at least they had so far.

"How about something different tonight?" Scott asked, as they walked hand-in-hand out of class.

"What did you have in mind?"

"Dinner at my place. I'm cooking."

An electric current ran through Madison's body. In the month they'd been going out, more or less officially, they'd only made out so far, but going to Scott's house could mean a lot more would happen tonight. Madison quickly did a mental checklist of her legs and bikini waxing status… *Phew, all good.*

"You can cook?" she asked.

"A very limited set of dishes."

"So what's on the menu tonight?"

"I can make a mean steak."

Madison lifted up on her tiptoes and gave him a quick peck on the lips. "How mean?"

Inside Scott's apartment, Madison rubbed her hands together to warm them up. February was almost over, but the weather didn't appear to be improving. The temperature was still in the low thirties, and it had snowed again only two days ago.

Scott hugged her from behind and, pushing her hair out of the way, he pressed his lips to her neck in a soft kiss. "Cold?" he asked.

The kiss spread a warm fuzz through her from the tips of her ears down to her frozen toes. Madison leaned back into him. "Not really… Not anymore."

At that, he spun her around and kissed her properly. Things heated up pretty fast, and soon

Madison found herself pressed against the wall, burning hot inside her coat. All she wanted was to get rid of the several layers of clothing separating her and Scott and really touch him, skin on skin.

"Err-hem," someone coughed to their left.

Scott pulled back at once, and Madison stared up at him in confusion for a while, as if emerging from a daze. Then she turned her head to the left, where Jack was standing. He was looking at them with half a smirk—part embarrassed, and part male comradeship.

"Sorry guys," Jack said. "I would've let you carry on, but you're basically blocking the door."

Both Madison and Scott quickly moved out of the hallway, leaving the path free for Jack.

"You going out?" Scott asked.

"Yeah, I'm seeing Alice," Jack said. Then, with a knowing little grin, he added, "Probably going to spend the night. You guys have a good time." And he was gone.

Butterflies exploded in Madison's belly. They'd be here alone all night.

Scott hung his coat and cleared his throat. "So, dinner…"

Madison followed his example by hanging her coat next to his and joined him in the open kitchen. "Yeah, you have to show me this special recipe of yours."

Scott opened a bottle of red wine, and Madison

sat on the counter, far away enough from the stove so that oil wouldn't spritz on her. She admired Scott's kitchen skills as she sipped her wine. The steaks didn't take long to cook and, after helping him set the table, they sat down to eat.

"Mmm," Madison moaned at her first bite of steak. It was juicy and seasoned to perfection. "One of the best steaks I've ever had."

Scott lowered his fork. "One of?"

Madison smiled. "Okay, the best."

One bottle of wine and one delicious steak later, Scott became suddenly serious.

"There's something I want to ask you," he said.

"Go ahead." Madison braced herself for whatever was about to come out of his mouth. Judging from the Heathcliff frown, it was nothing good.

"David." Scott stalled for a few seconds. "How did he know about your feelings for me?"

Madison's face flared with heat. She already was the blushing type, and after several glasses of wine, it got ten times worse. "Good intuition, I guess?"

"Why would you confide in him?"

"I didn't. But when he flat-out asked, I couldn't really deny it."

"So you two talk often?"

Madison shifted in her chair. She was about to reply when Scott spoke again. "Should I open another bottle of wine?"

"Yes, please," Madison said.

More wine was essential if they were having the "David" conversation.

Scott got up and was back in no time with an unopened bottle. Damn, he was sexy as he worked the corkscrew. The cork came out with a loud pop, and Scott refilled both their glasses.

After they'd both taken generous sips, Scott spoke again. "I'm sorry for the third degree," he said, smiling. "But given recent events… I need to understand what the deal is with you and my brother."

"Fair enough…" Madison nodded. "I guess you could say we're friends."

"Friends? You two were dating last year…"

"Yeah, for a couple of months. He was a total douche, though, so no regrets there."

"But if he was a douche, how can you be his friend?"

"I told you he apologized… and he can be pretty convincing." Madison wasn't sure how to make Scott understand. "We sort of bonded over the situation, you know? He was in love with Haley, I was in love with—" Madison stopped talking, aghast at what she'd been about to say.

Scott's emerald green eyes sparkled. "With me?" he asked.

"You can't ask me that on a third date."

Madison scoffed.

"If you consider the first unofficial three, it's our sixth…"

"This isn't fair. You already know more than you should! And I can't tell you how I feel after such a short time."

"Why not?"

"Because guys run away from strong feelings, and they don't want to hear how completely obsessed a girl is with them. I'm supposed to play hard to get here…"

"You're so cute when you blush," Scott said. "Did I ever tell you that?"

Madison's cheeks burned. "Oh, you're having fun, aren't you?"

"Yes." He flashed her another grin before turning serious again. "Madison, I spent the last four months of my last relationship like an unwanted guest in my own house. I was with a girl that wasn't just playing hard to get; she *was* hard to get. And it was exhausting. All the doubts, the second-guessing, the jealousy… So, I wish my next girlfriend to tell me exactly how strong her feelings for me are, and how completely obsessed she is with me."

"In short, you want a full confession."

Scott nodded and stared at her. Madison stalled, taking another sip of wine. What he was asking her to do was relationship suicide. He wanted her to lay her heart bare, while he still hadn't even admitted to anything more than liking her. Madison was seriously tempted to keep her mouth shut. But what would that accomplish? Yeah, she'd save face, but then she'd just keep on being miserable. It had been so hard to conceal her feelings this past year, and now she had an opportunity to let it all out. And if Scott laughed in her face… well, then, she knew the drill: *Stay strong and pull through.*

"Okay." Madison dropped her glass on the table and stared up at Scott. "I've had a crush on you since you walked into McDougall's class freshman year."

Scott's lips parted in a goofy smile. "Really?"

"Yeah. You had the full attention of the female population the second you walked in. Let's just say that tall guys of the basketball playing kind are not that common in poetry classes. And then… remember our first assignment?"

"The sonnet?"

"Mm-hmm. You wrote that piece about water…" Madison rehearsed the first few lines. "My cold water, you inspire me to write. How I hate the way you flow, lap and rush."

"Invading my mind day and through the night," Scott recited the next line of the first quatrain with her. "How do you even remember that?"

"I used to annotate all poems, and I liked yours the most… so my crush became certified."

"But you never said more than 'hi' to me."

Madison shrugged. "I'm shy. I don't talk to guys…"

"Okay, go on…"

"Isn't this enough?"

"Nuh-uh." Scott smiled devilishly. "I want the whole story."

Madison took another sip of wine. "Last year, when Alice was dating Peter, we started going to Lavietes to watch the games with her. Watching you play was… did I ever tell you how good you look in a basketball uniform?"

"Just now, I think." He winked.

Madison smiled, but then her brain moved on to the next phase.

"What's with the sad face?"

"Well, the next part of the story starts at Christmas…"

She held Scott's gaze and recognized the shadow passing behind his eyes.

"When Alice asked us to go with her to Hawaii, I wanted to go, but my family is… complicated. My grandparents are big on Christmas, and I couldn't go. But I had this irrational fear that something would happen between you and Haley… and it did."

"Did she know how you…?"

"No, not back then. Alice had guessed it, and she was the only person I could talk to for a long time. And that's also when things got worse…"

Scott frowned.

"Before, you were only a guy in my class I had a silly crush on. But when you started dating Haley, we all started going out together, and I got to know you better… That's also when you started sitting next to me in class, when we started saying something beyond 'hi' to each other, and I fell more and more for you."

"But you were already dating David back then."

"The first night I went home with David was also the first night I saw you and Haley together. I drank more than I should have, and David was there, as broody as I was. He noticed me, and… I knew it wasn't right, but you know when you want to do something specifically because it's the wrong thing?"

Scott nodded.

"That was me that night. But dating David didn't mean I couldn't still think about you."

"And when did Haley find out about… you know?" He gestured between them.

"At the end of the school year. I got into a huge fight with Alice, and since she was mad at me, she spilled the beans to Haley."

"She never said a word."

"Because I asked her not to. And, Scott, it was hard on her. It wasn't fair of me to ask her to keep secrets from you, and she's felt guilty about dating you from the moment she found out about me. She must've hated not being able to tell you why, but she did it anyway because she's my best friend."

They both stood silent for a while.

"I know the period you're talking about," Scott eventually said. "A few things make more sense now. Why did you break up with David?"

"We got into a stupid fight, and he was dating me only to make Haley jealous."

Scott's jaw tensed.

"Don't get mad at him for that. I was dating him to get over you, so I wasn't really any better. And he's already apologized for everything he did."

"Well, not to me."

"No, but when enough time has passed, give him a chance. I know he's impossible, but, Scott, he loves you. The day you got into a fight at Blake's house he was heartbroken over Haley, but the moment it seemed you were about to get yourself involved in a brawl, he was there by your side to back you up. And when they pushed you into the pool... You should've seen him. He dove right in and pulled you out, and..."

"Saved my life."

"Exactly. When it looked like you weren't

breathing, he lost it. I've never seen anyone so desperate. That wasn't a lie."

There was another long silence as Madison gathered the courage to ask him to clear the doubts she still had about them. His turn to be honest…

"Are you… are you really sorry about any of what David did? I mean, I know he's not in the running for brother of the year, but if he hadn't lied to you about kissing Haley, you wouldn't have gone to California… and now you would…"

"…still be dating her," Scott finished.

"Is that what you'd prefer? To be with Haley?"

Scott stood up and rounded the table, taking one of Madison's hands and pulling her up. He pushed her hair behind her shoulders and cupped her cheeks. Then, looking her straight into the eyes, he said, "There's nowhere else I'd rather be tonight… with no one else." He kissed her. "You know when was the first time that I realized the world would keep on spinning after Haley and I broke up?"

"No."

Scott ran his hands down her arms and wrapped them behind her back. "That afternoon with you in the library. You made everything better. Being around you felt… right. Since David told me about you having feelings for me, I haven't been able to push you out of my head, and I've never felt more wanted or serene than I do with you. Madison, we've been classmates, then friends, and now… you're my rock. I spent the last month waiting for our Wednesday nights together… You're smart, beautiful, kind…"

Did anyone have a fire extinguisher? Because Madison was sure her face was on fire.

Scott nuzzled the tip of his nose against the tip of hers. He leaned in to kiss her, but Madison pulled back.

"I know I've said a lot of things tonight, and I don't want to rush us, but if you want to run for the hills, this is probably your moment."

Scott pulled her close again. "I'm not going anywhere. So, that's it? You've left nothing out?"

Madison bit her lower lip. "Jack London isn't really my favorite author."

Scott's eyes widened. "But we've discussed all his books. You know them almost by heart!"

Madison smiled shyly. "Well, after I told you I liked him, I had to read them… didn't I?"

"I can live with that," he said with a foxy grin, before killing any further conversation with another kiss.

Scott scooped Madison up in his arms and carried her to his room, where he laid her on the bed. He climbed on top of her and stopped to look at her. "You're so beautiful," he whispered.

And as he leaned his head down to kiss her again, there was nothing or no one holding them back. They'd laid everything out in the open, and even if neither of them had said the three magic words—I love you—they shared a connection so deep it didn't need to be expressed in words.

Making love with Scott overwhelmed Madison in ways she wasn't prepared to handle. Her emotions ran so deep that tears rolled down her cheeks. He didn't mock her about it, or shy away; he kissed her tears and made her feel like the most beautiful and wanted woman in the world. He made her feel loved, he made her feel finally home…

Twenty-two
Ethan

Three Months Later

"Can you hold her?" Georgiana dropped a smiling Jane into Ethan's lap and went to join the queue of new graduates.

Ethan stared dubiously into the baby's eyes, not sure he was up to babysitting her for the duration of the graduation ceremony. But then his niece smiled at him, and Ethan found himself cooing over her like a mother hen.

Lifting his gaze, he caught Rose staring at him with an amused smirk.

"Baby looks good on you," she mouthed from across the podium where she was waiting with the other graduates for the ceremony to start.

Ethan stuck out his tongue, which earned him an enthusiastic chuckle from baby Jane. So he bounced the baby on his knees to make her laugh louder.

When he looked back up at the line of grad students waiting to receive their diplomas, his eyes drifted to Rose's left hand, and to the engagement ring he'd given her at Christmas. In three months, she'd be his wife. A proud smile surfaced on his lips. He sure was a lucky bastard.

Next, his eyes wandered to his sister's naked hand. No wedding band there, same as Tyler. Becoming a mom had changed Georgiana so much that Ethan hardly recognized her sometimes. She'd matured and stopped acting like a spoiled princess. In just a few months, she'd grown up enough to face her mistakes. She and Tyler had agreed they were wonderful parents, but terrible at being husband and wife. They'd be divorced by the end of the year.

Ethan stared at his soon to be ex-brother-in-law, wanting to hate the dude for everything he'd done to Georgiana. But he finally had to admit his sister shared a big part of the responsibility, and... If it weren't for Tyler, Ethan would've never met Rose, and now he wouldn't be holding this bundle of joy in his arms.

Ethan stared into Jane's blue eyes—his eyes, Georgiana's eyes. The past two years had been a mess for his sister, but she'd still managed to graduate on time and give birth to the most beautiful baby in the world... and now she could find someone who really loved her, someone who deserved her and who would make her happy.

And, yeah, Tyler, too. Provided he kept away from Rose.

Some things never changed, after all…

A professor walked on stage and grabbed the microphone to kick off the ceremony. Ethan settled back in his chair and whispered in Jane's ear, "Look, your mom, your dad, and your aunt-to-be are all about to graduate."

Baby Jane replied with a satisfied, "Ghe-ghe-gwakh."

David

David adjusted the angle of his phone, orienting the camera to include everyone in the picture. Five people stared back at him through the lenses, all dressed the same in their black regalia and caps.

To the left, Scott kept an arm wrapped around Madison's waist, as did Jack with Alice to the right. And in the middle, one arm around each of her roommates' shoulders, was Haley. The girl who'd stolen his heart almost two years ago on a starry summer night.

"Say 'cheese!'" David yelled, snapping away on the phone's camera. "Hang on, let me change the angle."

He shifted to the left, and the five new graduates rotated their ranks with him to stay in front of the camera.

"Okay." David stopped. "Now say, 'David's so handsome.'" He snapped another shot and grinned as he looked at the picture flashing on his screen.

Scott, wearing a half-exasperated smirk. Madison, rolling her eyes. Jack and Alice, staring into each other's eyes, smiling, and not giving a crap about him. And Haley, her lips pursed to blow him a kiss, her green eyes sparkling with joy in the sun.

Note From The Author

Dear Reader,

I hope you enjoyed *I Don't Want To Be Friends*. Thank you so much for following the series to the end! I'm not saying this will be the last book in the series ever, but it will be for a while. Rose, Tyler, Ethan, Georgiana, Madison, Alice, Haley, Jack, David, and Scott all want to say, "Thank you, and goodbye."

If you loved their story, **please leave a review** on Goodreads, your favorite retailer's website, or wherever you like to post reviews (your blog, your Facebook wall, your bedroom wall, in a text to your best friend…). Reviews are the best gift you can give to an author, and word of mouth is the most powerful means of book discovery.

If you're craving more romance, you can turn the page for an excerpt from *Love Connection,* the first book in my romantic comedy series *First Comes Love*.

Thank you for your support!

Camilla, x

Sneak Peek: Love Connection

One

Two Weddings

Saturday, June 10—New York, JFK Airport

"You've been staring at those two plane tickets for almost an hour now. My role as bartender compels me to ask: what's the big dilemma?"

I stare at the guy behind the bar for the first time since I sat on this stool an hour ago. He has a broad smile and a friendly face.

"If you stop pretending to be drying glasses just to peek at my tickets and pour me another drink," I say, "I'll tell you."

"Sambuca, with ice?"

I nod and shift my attention back to my tickets. Maybe if I stare at them hard enough, the letters will magically move and spell out a solution for me. In the background, I can hear ice tinkle as it hits the bottom of a glass, then crack when the bartender pours the Sambuca. These sounds mingle with the general noises of the airport: flight announcements, passengers chatting, and luggage rolling on the floor.

"Here you go." The bartender sets my drink on the glassy surface of the bar in front of me.

"You added coffee beans," I observe. "Nice touch."

"Pleased to please. But isn't 7 a.m. a little too early for double heavy spirits?"

"I'm on U.K. time, and believe me, I need the double heavy spirits."

"Which brings us back to the tickets. I've earned an explanation."

I sip my Sambuca and take a closer look at the guy's face. Young—mid-twenties, I'd say. Short sandy hair, intelligent eyes, and always the big smile. He's back at his occupation of drying glasses that don't need drying. Probably one of those people incapable of standing still with nothing to do.

On the screen behind him, a report about a fire at Miami International Airport is taking over the news. The screen reads that the fire has been contained with no casualties, but the airport will sustain heavy delays throughout the day.

"Looks like they're having troubles in Miami," I say, jerking my chin toward the screen.

"Trying to change the subject, are we? You're not going to make me beg for your story, are you?"

I swirl the ice in my glass. "Is this on the house?"

"On the house, along with the free advice."

"All right. One ticket's for San Francisco, the other one for Chicago. There're two weddings today, and I need to choose which one to go to."

"Two close friends?"

"You could say that."

"Oh, okay. Let's see, do you have a particular role in one of the weddings? I mean, do both your friends expect you to show up? Don't you usually need to RSVP months in advance for this kind of thing?"

"Mmm, this wedding…" I push the Chicago ticket forward. "I'm supposed to be the maid of honor. This wedding…" I slide the San Francisco ticket next to its twin on the countertop. "I'm not invited."

The bartender snorts. "Seems pretty straightforward to me. Why would you want to bail on a friend to go to a wedding you're not invited to?"

I look him in the eyes. "To stop it from happening."

"Woo-oh. And the plot thickens. My morning just got a lot more interesting than I was expecting. Is it about a guy? Is he the one who got away?"

"Yep." I take another swig of Sambuca; it burns my throat as I swallow. "You don't make burgers here, by any chance? I'm starving."

"Burgers at seven in the morning?"

"I told you, I'm on U.K. time. And burgers are my favorite."

"Sorry, but the kitchen's closed. I can give you some tortilla chips." He opens a new bag and pours them into a wooden bowl. "So, what's his name?"

"Jake."

"Jake." The bartender pauses. "The name has appeal."

"Not just the name." I sigh.

"You want to tell me what happened?"

"We first dated in high school. After graduation, he wanted to go to Stanford, and I wanted to go to Harvard."

The bartender whistles. "The war of the Ivy Leagues. What do you guys do?"

"I'm a lawyer. He's a surgeon."

"So what happened? You fought over schools, went your separate ways, and drifted apart during college?" he asks, his tone saying, *"Same old, same old."*

"No. I went to Stanford instead, to be with him. He assured me we'd go to Harvard for grad school."

"Oh. I sense that promise didn't come true. So

you stayed together through college as well. And…?"

"Stanford offered him a scholarship for Med School. Everything paid for. No student loans, no living expenses. It was an offer no one could've refused."

"And that's when you broke up?"

"No, not yet. I hadn't applied to Stanford Grad School, so for me, it was either lose one year or move to Boston. Harvard was my dream, Stanford his. It wouldn't have been fair for either of us to have to give up our dream school."

"So you left?"

"Yeah. We spent the summer in California and I moved to Boston at the beginning of the fall term. We thought three years apart would be manageable. That's when we found out why everyone says long distance relationships don't work. School was demanding for both of us and catching a six-hour flight over the weekend became more and more difficult. We settled on leading different lives. We were used to sharing everything. Every day, every moment. Suddenly, we both had this huge chunk of life with different things in it. Things the other couldn't understand or get excited about. It was hard. We started arguing, and…"

"And?"

"Depends who you ask. If you asked Jake, he'd

probably tell you it was a miscommunication issue. He'd say I overreacted to him telling me about a job offer he'd received in San Francisco. If you asked me, I'd give you a slightly different version…"

"Was your career really that important?" the bartender asks.

"It wasn't that I valued my career over my relationship with Jake. It was the sensation of always coming in second after *his* career. I'd given up my college dream for him. I'd waited all of graduate school… it was his turn to put me first. To put *us* first."

"If he's still in San Francisco, what's made you change your mind now about being together?"

"I'm not sure I *have* changed my mind."

"So why buy a ticket to San Francisco if you're not even sure you want to try to work things out with him?"

"It was a rash, stupid decision. When I found out Jake was getting married, I panicked. My first thought was that I couldn't let him do it."

"So what's changed?"

"I cooled off and thought about it."

"And?"

"And I realized flying to San Francisco and confronting him was crazy. I mean, what are the odds, really, of us getting back together? I live in London, and he lives in San Francisco. I haven't seen him in forever. I know nothing about his life. We ruined everything once already. How can we possibly make it work this time?"

"And yet here you are, staring at a ticket to San Francisco and contemplating crashing his wedding."

"I can't stop asking myself the 'what if?' question. I'm tired of living in a world of what ifs."

"Meaning?"

"I might've been a tad unreasonable after our break up," I admit.

"As in?"

"As in I moved to the other side of the world and ignored all his calls, emails, and messages. I wanted a fresh start, so I cut him out completely."

The bartender grabs the now-empty wooden bowl and refills it with tortilla chips. "Why?" he asks.

"I was sure he could talk me into moving back to San Francisco if I gave him the chance."

"And you didn't want to quit your job for him?"

"I couldn't. I owed it to myself to make the best choice for *my* career. But the fact remains that moving to the other side of the world didn't help much in forgetting him. I'm still in love with him. He's the only one I ever loved."

"How long ago was this?"

"Three years."

"And you haven't seen him or spoken to him since then?"

"I'm a mess, I know."

"How did you find out he was getting married?"

"Amelia told me—my best friend, the other one getting married today. Amelia, Jake and I are all from a small town near Chicago. She moved to London after getting her bachelor degree and she lives there with her soon-to-be-husband William. But she wanted to get married at home. Anyway, Amelia and Jake had some guests in common, they told Amelia about Jake's wedding as they'd already RSVP'd 'Yes' to him."

"Do you know the girl he's marrying?"

"No." I shake my head decisively. "I don't know anything about her, and I've forced myself not to search Google for intel."

"Aren't you curious?"

"*Yes*. But I can't give her a face. I'd never be able to crash her wedding if I did. She has to stay a ghost."

"When are the weddings?"

"This afternoon."

"Whoa. What's so special about June 10 that everyone wants to get married today? And you're hard-core. Shouldn't you have tried to talk to the guy a little sooner? Are you literally going to barge into the church and yell 'STOP!' in the middle of the ceremony?"

"I'd decided not to go at all."

"But you brought the ticket all the way from London, just in case."

"I did. Having the ticket, even if I knew I wasn't going to use it, made me feel calmer."

"And now you've changed your mind?"

"I don't know. I have no idea what I'm doing."

"When does the plane leave?"

"Which one?"

"Tell me both times."

"San Francisco's eight thirty. Chicago's ten forty-five."

"So you have less than…" He pauses to look at his watch. "Twenty minutes before they start boarding for San Francisco."

"That's correct."

"What's Amelia's take on the situation?"

"She got mad at me at first for even thinking about ditching her wedding. But then again, she's always been a huge fan of Gemma and Jake."

"Gemma?"

"That's me. We all grew up on the same street, and we've been friends forever. Anyway, she's marshaled a back-up maid of honor and she told me to follow my heart."

"And what does your heart say?"

"My heart's telling me it loves Jake. But this is

too big. As you said, I can't run into the church and beg him to cancel the wedding."

"What time's the wedding?"

"Six p.m."

"What time does your plane land?"

I look at the ticket. "Noon."

"So you'd have plenty of time to get there before the ceremony starts."

"Mmm, I'm not so sure. The wedding's in some fancy winery in Napa."

"That's barely an hour's drive. You'll still have all the time you need to get there and talk to him before he goes to the altar."

"But what am I going to say?"

"Say that you love him."

"And?"

"Nothing else. If he's in love with you, it'll be enough."

"Say he doesn't laugh in my face and tell me to leave. Say he admits he still loves me. It doesn't change anything. I'm still in London, and he's still in San Francisco."

"You'll figure something."

"I'm not so sure."

"You said it yourself: you don't want to live in a world of what ifs, right? So it seems pretty obvious you have to try."

"But I'm so scared."

"Do you have anything to lose?"

"No, not really."

"Then why not go?"

"What if he doesn't love me anymore?"

"Then he doesn't, and it will suck, but at least you'll have your answer. But if you don't go, and you don't ask, you'll never know, and you'll regret it for the rest of your life. If you love him, go."

My face becomes suddenly hot and an electric prickle spreads from my heart to my fingertips. "Right. What's the worst that could happen?"

"They could arrest you for crashing a private party. Or the bride could sue you for emotional damages. Or…"

"I'm a lawyer; I can take care of myself in the law department. Are you on my side or what?"

"Of course I am. So, what's the next step?"

"A car. I'm going to need a car in San Francisco. I need to rent a car." My pulse is racing. I pick up my phone and tap away frantically. "Uhhuuuhhhu. It's done. I did it. I've booked a car. I'm really doing this. Oh gosh. I'm doing it! Is it too lame if I want to high five you?"

"No, not at all." He raises his palm. "Shoot away."

I slam my hand into his. "I have to tell Amelia so she can get her maid-of-honor-plan-B rolling."

"All passengers. Flight UA 730, with destination San Francisco, is beginning boarding

at gate B 25. We're going to start boarding families with small kids and passengers with special needs. Then, we're going to board first and business class passengers. And finally, all other passengers…"

"That's your flight they just announced."

"It's my flight. I'm going." I fumble with my bag and carry-on luggage and almost fall from the stool. "How much do I owe you?"

"It's on the house."

"Everything?"

"Yeah. You go tell your man you love him. Go catch your love connection."

"Thank you. Thank you so much." I hurry toward the gate.

"Hey," the bartender calls after me. "Let me know how it goes! I'm on Facebook."

"What's your name?" I shout back without stopping.

"I'm Mark Cooper. And you?"

"Gemma Dawson."

Acknowledgments

The first huge thank you goes to my street team. I've only just created this group a few months ago, and your support has already been overwhelming.

Thank you to all my readers. Without your constant support, I wouldn't keep pushing through the blank pages.

Thank you to my editors and proofreaders, Michelle Proulx, Helen Baggott, and Jennifer Harris for making my writing the best it could be.

And lastly, thank you to my family and friends for your constant encouragement.

Cover and Interior Image Credit: Created by Freepik